DIM LIGHTS THICK SMOKE

*A Northern Arizona Crime Novel
Featuring Edison Graves*

Trevor Holliday

Barnstork Press

Copyright © 2021 Trevor Holliday

All rights reserved

The characters and events portrayed in this book are fictitious. Any similarity to real persons, living or dead, is coincidental and not intended by the author.

No part of this book may be reproduced, or stored in a retrieval system, or transmitted in any form or by any means, electronic, mechanical, photocopying, recording, or otherwise, without express written permission of the publisher.

ISBN-13: 9798587647022
ISBN-10: 1477123456

Cover design by: John Holliday
Library of Congress Control Number: 2018675309
Printed in the United States of America

Dedicated to the people of Holbrook, Arizona.

WAITING FOR SUNRISE

Edison Graves stood barefoot in the desert, three miles from Globe, Arizona. Each one of Edison's morning runs took him along the four points of a compass.

Running aligned Edison's spirit with his body. Today, Edison's run would take him south. The sun would rise on his right side and would be on his left when he returned.

Old Joe Beach told Edison to follow this procedure to keep his life in order.

Joe Beach was well known on the rez. He was Apache, but he'd married a Navajo wife. Joe's wife was long gone, but Joe still lived just a little north of Holbrook, a few miles into the Navajo Nation.

Joe Beach claimed to have known Chief Alchesay. Joe met him when he was young, long after the legendary Apache chief earned the Medal of Honor in the Indian Wars. Edison heard Joe tell the story a few times. The basics of the story were consistent, but Edison had his doubts.

Could Joe ever have met Chief Alchesay? Alchesay had died in 1928.

Joe was old, no doubt. His hair was gray, his wrinkles were deep. His teeth and his vision were all but gone. But Joe Beach wasn't *that* old. Not *nearly* that old.

Still, Edison couldn't fault the old man for embroidering his own legend.

Joe helped Edison many times in his life. After Edison's parents were killed, Joe sheltered Edison and his younger brother until Livingston arrived. After Livingston was killed last year, Joe helped Edison through the ensuing chaos. Joe's healing ceremony helped Edison regain harmony.

Joe was Merlinda Beach's grandfather. Edison still thought about Merlinda. They had dated while they were in high school. Edison wondered if Merlinda had ever left Holbrook.

The sky was dark. Edison started his morning run before sunrise, a purple ridge stretching across the line of the horizon from the north to the south.

Thoughts crossed through Edison's mind. Edison knew he owed much to people who had helped him through the years. Livingston and Tasha. Joe Beach.

Frank Trinity in Tucson had also helped Edison and Edison had since visited Trinity to thank him.

Repeating the simple words taught to him by Joe Beach, Edison breathed in the desert air. Edison loved the earthy scent of the morning hours and the sight of the sagebrush and cholla.

CONTENTS

Title Page
Copyright
Dedication
Waiting for Sunrise　　　　　　　　　　2
The Sunset Motel　　　　　　　　　　　5
Cheerleader's Smile　　　　　　　　　 16
Tilt-a-Whirl　　　　　　　　　　　　　20
First Phase Dine'　　　　　　　　　　 22
Miracle Mile　　　　　　　　　　　　　30
Cold Pizza at the Sunset Motel　　　　 33
Antonio's Revenge　　　　　　　　　　44
Johnny Angel Knocked Him Out　　　 53
Sweat-Stained Guayaberra　　　　　　61
Legends of the West　　　　　　　　　64
Pedal Steel　　　　　　　　　　　　　 67
No Better Mexican Food　　　　　　　71
Sunset and Neon　　　　　　　　　　 77

County Courthouse	80
Bigger Fish	84
Mama Tried	89
Lonesome Buckaroos	93
The Model 10	96
Green, Green Grass of Home	101
The Stagecoach Steak House	103
The Ten High Saloon	110
Pay Phone	121
The Next Teardrop	123
Pawn Shop	129
Identical Bartenders	131
Heading Toward Route 66	134
Chloral Hydrate	137
Other Voices	139
Red and White Ford F-150	140
The Metal Parts of the Shotgun	144
Past the Bucket of Blood	147
The Dying Art of Safecracking	151
Hell in its Day	154
Dirty Money	156
Adobe Walls and Plywood on the Windows	158
D-I-V-O-R-C-E	162
The Hitchhiker	165

Bakersfield	170
The Deserted Midway of the County Fairground	172
The Paint	178
Enchiladas	180
A Plume of Smoke	183
Permission	185
Books By This Author	188
Acknowledgement	190

TREVOR HOLLIDAY

He thought about Merlinda Beach.

Edison repeated Joe's words every morning on his desert run. The run would last four hours. Edison maintained a persistent, pounding pace. His bare feet, calloused by the hot caliche of the desert, were immune to the trail's hazards. The first hour of the run his mind was active. In the second hour, distractions always left him.

Two hours after starting, Edison turned back toward the trailer.

The orange glimmer of the sun's corona peeked over the horizon. The red ball climbed into the sky over the town of Globe, returning life to the world after night's deep dark death.

In the distance, Edison saw the copper mine where he worked. The place was shut down and would be for a while.

THE SUNSET MOTEL

James Locaster's voice made Dallas King's skin crawl. It was early for a phone call from Locaster. Dallas stood in the office of the Sunset Motel in Holbrook, Arizona.

The Sunset was his own motel. Dallas had bought it with cash. He was six foot two inches tall standing in his crew socks. He wore longish blond hair, parted on the side. A hint of Vitalis, but nothing greasy.

People said Dallas looked like Glen Campbell.

The Sunset consisted of four painted concrete tepees, an office, and a pool Dallas knew he should either clean or empty. Behind the tepees, a concrete annex of rooms stood in disrepair. A permanent sign in front of the Sunset read VACANCIES.

Three vintage cars were parked in front of the tepees. Dallas parked them there to make it look like business, even when the place was empty.

Dallas paid cash for the motel. In return, he expected cash payment for the rooms.

He was thinking of installing a Tilt-a-Whirl in the parking lot. Dallas knew how to run them. Small carnival rides made money.

❋ ❋ ❋

"Hey, surfer boy," Locaster said. "Tonight's the night, am I right? You ready to make some dinero? The thing we been talking about, right?"

Locaster was right. Tonight was the night. They *had* been talking about it.

Dallas had put cheese into the trap and now the rat was coming to feast upon it.

Locaster was the rat.

Dallas was desperate for Locaster's wife to leave Locaster.

Locaster wasn't the only one calling Dallas. Wanda made calls to Dallas, too. She had been making the calls every week from wherever she and Locaster were staying.

"Collect call, from Wanda Locaster," the operator would say. "Do you accept the charges?"

You better believe Dallas accepted those charges. Wanda kept saying how she was ready to leave Locaster.

Dallas had plenty of money, even after buying the Sunset Motel. He told Wanda about the money in his safe. He had put his cash away just for the two of them.

Dallas looked out the plate glass window at the

traffic going west.

Tonight, he thought.

❋ ❋ ❋

Hearing Locaster on the phone got under Dallas's skin. Even though Dallas knew Locaster would call, the sound of his voice put him on edge. Dallas knew he needed to get himself under control.

Dallas had designed the plan.

He had mentioned his cousin Tony's pawn shop to Locaster long ago. Soon after the two had met.

The first few weeks of their association, Dallas had said a lot of things to Locaster and Wanda. At first he had been trying to impress Locaster. Later he wanted to impress Wanda.

Locaster took the bait. He was very interested in the pawn shop.

"Sure, tonight's the night, James," Dallas said. "Look, I got it set up. You gotta remember Tony's armed to the teeth. He doesn't go anywhere without a gun. And he's mean, too. It doesn't take much to provoke him. But he's got cash. He doesn't believe in banks."

Dallas didn't believe in banks either.

The plan was complicated, and required good timing, but Locaster had agreed.

Dallas couldn't believe Locaster took the bait.

❊ ❊ ❊

Locaster sounded irritated.

"You told me, Dallas. You told me. You have explained all of this to me. Over and over. All I need to know is if you're ready. Because, we got one thing he don't. We got the element of surprise. Think he's expecting anything?"

Dallas looked at the receiver. Typical for Locaster to turn the tables on Dallas.

"James," Dallas said, "you need to know who we're dealing with. I've known Tony all my life."

"So you told me. Now I'm asking *you* something. Are *you* ready? Because once me and Wanda start up that road, there's no coming back. You know those nukes they got pointing at Russia from submarines? We're the nukes. The president himself can't call those nukes back."

Dallas felt sweat under his arms. He didn't like perspiring. Wanda was coming up. The only thing he wanted her to smell on him was Aqua Velva Ice Blue.

Dallas hoped he was being tricky enough. There were two parts of the plan he needed to put together. He felt like a juggler spinning plates on Ed Sullivan. He wasn't worried, though. Dallas knew once those plates were in the air they would spin.

"Course I'm ready, James. It's not a question of *me* being ready."

The long distance call wasn't good quality. Locaster sounded like he was calling from the bottom of a well instead of from a phone booth outside his motel room in Tucson.

Wanda had said she and Locaster were back in Tucson. Wanda told Dallas that Locaster was acting strangely.

He was paranoid about where she was going and what she was doing.

Locaster wanted to know every step she took.

Dallas understood Locaster's vigilance. He would have done the same in Locaster's shoes.

* * *

After their last job, Locaster said he was done working with Dallas, but Wanda kept calling Dallas, and Dallas came up with the plan. He told Wanda to remind Locaster about the pawn shop.

Just remind him.

Dallas didn't want Locaster to know Wanda was calling him.

Dallas couldn't figure out why Locaster had gone back to Tucson so soon after the strip club job. Going back anywhere near Tucson was risky as hell, and Locaster didn't like risk. You should *never* go back to the same place.

Before Wanda told him they were in Tucson, Dallas thought they were in El Paso or someplace.

Someplace other than Tucson.

New Mexico? Maybe.

Old Mexico would have been better, except

Wanda wouldn't have been able to call Dallas as easily.

But not Tucson. Tucson wasn't smart at all. Then staying at a place down on Miracle Mile?

What the hell was Locaster thinking?

❉ ❉ ❉

Wanda called Dallas every week.

Dallas liked the way she called to see if he was okay.

Wanda made Dallas feel better. She always got around to telling Dallas how much she wanted to be with him and not Locaster.

"I don't know how much longer I can deal with him," she said the last time she called.

It didn't do any good for Dallas to tell her to leave Locaster. Wanda was frightened of Locaster for good reason.

"Don't worry, baby," Dallas said. "It won't be much longer."

❉ ❉ ❉

When they first met, things were different between Dallas and Locaster.

Dallas had been able to put up with Locaster. He liked him, even. But Dallas had fallen hard for Wanda and it hadn't gotten better over time. It got worse.

Thinking about Locaster with Wanda now was almost enough to make Dallas throw up.

✻ ✻ ✻

Locaster raised his voice on the phone.

"You there, Dallas?" Locaster's voice was mean. "You spacing out, Dallas?"

"I'm here," Dallas said.

"Good thing," Locaster said. He laughed. "It sounded like you were getting cold feet or something. It's the sound of your voice, Dallas. You sound like you're getting scared."

Dallas shook his head.

"It's not like that, James."

"Whatever you say, Dallas. I'm just saying what it sounds like."

"No, I'm ready. It's on."

"That's good, Dallas. Just remember I took a chance on you. I was the one who taught you to do things right. That was me, Dallas. Your old buddy, James M. Locaster."

Locaster was a fool. Dallas didn't care about money. Dallas wanted Wanda.

Locaster wasn't going to bring Wanda up to Holbrook to look at the pretty rocks outside town.

Hell *no* he wasn't going to do that.

Locaster had to be lured.

"Fine, James," Dallas said. "Just come on up here. I'll give you and your lady Tepee Number Two. Best one I got."

"Number Two?" Locaster said. "Why not Number One?"

Whiny and sarcastic.

"Number One?" Dallas said. "You don't want that one."

Tepee Number One was Dallas's personal unit. Tepee Number One was special. First class all the way.

He and Wanda would live there once Locaster was out of the way.

Wanda would love the pink champagne in the fridge and the soft shag carpeting on the floor. He'd made it nice for her.

"Hey, surfer boy, one more thing."

"What's that, James?"

Locaster had lowered his voice.

Stupid, Dallas thought. Calling from a phone booth. Locaster was stupid in a lot of ways.

"I don't know what this other dude looks like. The Indian. Point him out to me. I'll get him riled up, you know what I mean?"

Dallas shook his head. What the hell was Locaster talking about? What was the purpose of getting Edison riled?

"Maybe I should put a sign on him or something, James? How about I pin a target on his back?"

"Don't get smart, Dallas. That's not like you. Just figure something out."

Dallas decided not to push things. Locaster was coming up and he was bringing Wanda.

Locaster had contacted Dallas shortly after Wanda reminded Locaster about the pawn shop.

Dallas knew his cousin Tony kept cash in the pawn shop safe. He would be glad to be rid of Tony. Tony was getting dangerous. He was asking Dallas too many questions.

Asking where Dallas had gotten the money to pay for the motel.

Tony was trouble.

Dallas could kill two birds with one stone.

Dallas had used that expression with Locaster once before about another job, but he'd gotten the saying wrong. Dallas had said they could kill a bird with two stones.

Dallas remembered Locaster laughing.

Locaster could be a supercilious son-of-a-bitch.

"One more thing," Locaster said.

Always one more thing with Locaster.

"What's that?"

"Same split as always. A third for me, a third for you. Wanda gets a third, too."

The split didn't make any difference to Dallas. He and Wanda would end up sharing anyway, but no sense making Locaster suspicious.

"James," Dallas said, "we gotta talk about this. If Wanda gets a share it's like you're taking two shares."

Dallas sounded whiny and he knew it, but it was part of the act.

"You sure about this guy?"

One more time, Locaster was asking about Edison Graves.

Locaster had said they needed a fall guy. Somebody to take the blame. Somebody who didn't know anything about the plan with the safe.

Dallas knew who to use.

"He's perfect," Dallas said. "He won't suspect nothing. He's gonna be busy with the girl I got for him."

"Just show me the guy. I'll take it from there."

"I'll show him to you, James."

"We'll do it the way we discussed then. Don't be stupid. Tell me now if you don't think it's gonna work."

"It'll work, James."

"You got things set with this guy? We can't come up on a maybe. We do that, we're back to square one, and James Locaster ain't gonna be happy."

"I got it lined up," Dallas said. "That's not the issue. But if it doesn't line up right, we gotta call it off. I gotta live here. I gotta business and a reputation."

"That's your problem, Dallas, your reputation. But it's the same split. I'm telling you now because I don't want you getting any ideas at the last minute. Wanda gets the same as both of us."

Dallas paused. As if he was thinking it over.

"This is different, James. I'm taking more risk here."

"No different, Dallas," Locaster said. "She gets the same."

Dallas nodded. Looked out at the street and across at the steak house.

Locaster thought Dallas objected to the split.

Dallas didn't care about the split. He couldn't have cared any less.

"What time you getting here?"

"We'll be there before dark. We're pulling out of here pretty soon."

"Tell you what. Gimme ten, fifteen minutes. Gimme a number where I can call you at if I can't get the guy. It don't work if I don't have the guy."

"Can't do that," Locaster said. "We start up there, we aren't turning around, even if old surfer boy says so. It don't work that way."

Locaster hung up.

Dallas put the phone down. Looked back out the window of the office.

He looked at the Rolodex next to the phone. Found the number and dialed.

CHEERLEADER'S SMILE

The guy behind the counter of the car place had been sweating. The polyester shirt he wore wasn't doing him any favors. Circles of perspiration had formed under his armpits. He waved his clipboard at Wanda. He'd been out on the lot when he saw her standing in the office.

"Inventory," he said. "It never ends, you know?"

She smiled.

"You must have a hundred cars out there," she said. "It must be hard."

The car rental guy hadn't been able to keep his eyes off Wanda. Locaster had sent her into the Ugly Duckling rent-a-car place on Oracle for the Mercury. He'd given her one of the credit cards he had gotten from a guy working at a place south of 22nd Street called *Taller Mechanico El Guapo*.

"Feel free to get yourself something nice with it, *after* you get the car," Locaster had said. "Use it for the car, get yourself something, then dump it."

She handed the guy the card Locaster had given her.

"Maroon's fine?" he said.

He handed her the keys. Pausing a little more than necessary. Giving her a look.

"Long as it's got air conditioning," she said.

She flashed her cheerleader's smile at the guy.

"They all got air conditioning," he said. "This is Tucson."

Not looking up. All business now.

"You're gonna want the supplemental insurance? Basic comes with comp and collision, you can get the loss damage waiver if you want." He paused. "I gotta ask. It's policy."

He tapped his pen. Looking her over now with a you-know-what-I-mean look.

Wanda cocked her head.

"I never know whether to do that or *not*. What do *you* think?"

The guy looked at her again. Pursing his lips. Making his mustache scrunch. The mustache didn't cover all the sweat on his upper lip. Coming in from the heat of the lot to the air conditioned office was making him sweat even more.

"Between you and me? Save your money. Course that's off the record. Kinda like high-test gas. Pretty much a ripoff."

Wanda nodded. All business while she signed. She glanced at the name on the card and wrote it the way it was spelled. *Mary Gonzales*. S was the last letter.

The car rental guy wasn't a bad guy, she thought. She looked up at him and winked.

"Take one of these," he said.

He handed her a cardboard air freshener.

"You like Pina Coladas?"

"Love them," Wanda said.

Laughed.

She gave him a good look at her legs when she left.

❈ ❈ ❈

Wanda had talked to Dallas.

"I got everything set up here nice for the two of us," Dallas had said.

Tell me about it," she had said.

"I know your favorite colors. Gold and pink, right? I got our place set up with those. You should see it. You're *gonna* see it, pretty soon."

She closed her eyes. She could imagine the place.

"Pink and gold and *green*. You did *that* for me?"

"Just for you, Wanda. Wait till you see it. It's gonna take your breath away, I swear."

"Dallas," she said. "Sounds like you knocked yourself out. You know James ran out of money, right? Almost right off the bat. We went to Laughlin. He was on a winning streak, you know? Then before you know it, he's asking me how much money I got. Like he gave *me* any money, you know? He didn't split it with me, Dallas. He just told you that. Most of what he got is gone."

"Wanda, I got plenty. I got it in a safe under the

hide-a-bar. Safe and sound."

"You think of everything, Dallas. I can't wait. I'm on pins and needles."

❋ ❋ ❋

Locaster opened the door slightly, tightening the security chain. Wanda saw his eyes and the glowing end of his Tiparillo. Wanda was used to the smell the thin cigars made in motel rooms where they stayed. The Fender case and the Samsonite were packed. She could see them through the crack. He opened the curtain maybe six inches, then opened the door just enough for Wanda to wedge inside.

The Tucson sun flooded the room.

"Why'd you get that color?" he said. "Looks like a pimpmobile."

"It's what they had, Jimmy. Don't be such a poop."

"I talked to Dallas," he said.

"Uh huh," she said. "That's good."

He picked up the Fender case in one hand and the Samsonite in the other. He turned to her.

"You need to use the ladies before we get going?"

Wanda shook her head.

"Thanks for asking, though."

TILT-A-WHIRL

Locaster looked at the rental Mercury parked in front of their room. It was a risk being in Tucson, but it was risky being anywhere.

Life was like a damned Tilt-a-Whirl, Locaster thought. Every ride on a Tilt-a-Whirl was different. It was a fact of nature, like snowflakes were all different. On the Tilt-a-Whirl you got your outward thrust and your upward lift. When the ride got going, there was no predicting what would happen except it would end. The mixing of the outward and upward forces was what made the ride both nauseating and irresistible. And no two rides were alike. Just like life.

He wasn't worried about the bikers.

They would be punished by their own people, and Locaster had been careful.

The strip club job had been quick, efficient, and profitable. More profitable than he'd believed it could be. Now Locaster had to be careful not to take unnecessary risks. No extra movement. Keeping away from contact with people who might know him.

He remembered looking at the cash spread out

over the table. Dallas had stared gape-mouthed. There was more cash than they had planned on. Way more. Somehow, they'd gotten themselves into something big.

"Feast your eyes," Locaster said to Dallas and Wanda, "You're never going to have a better day's work than this."

Mostly he had been speaking to Dallas.

Locaster knew it would be their last real job together. He had to admit, the three of them had made a good team. But you had to know when to call it quits.

❃ ❃ ❃

Wanda had gone out to the car to start the air conditioning. She had rolled down the window of the Mercury and her tanned right leg pointed toward the motel's pool. They had all made a good team until surfer boy got hot pants for Wanda.

Then it was over.

Locaster and Wanda would head north on Oracle toward the Catalina Mountains. In Locaster's business, retirement wasn't an option.

But he had to admit he felt a little tired.

FIRST PHASE DINE'

When Edison returned to the trailer, the sun was above the horizon and was beating down on his shoulders and back. The day would take whatever course it would take. The outside shower felt good on his body. He felt hot from the long run but the water stayed at a steady cool temperature. Not too cold. Just right.

Edison's day looked promising. The long runs made him feel alive and more in tune with the world.

It could be a perfect day.

Edison heard the phone ring inside the trailer after he finished warming up some frijoles. He scraped the last of the beans out of the splatterwear saucepan onto a tortilla, grabbed a block of cheese from the refrigerator and cut off a wedge to place on top of the beans before rolling the tortilla, beans, and cheese into a burro.

He didn't want to pick up the phone.

He put the burro into a skillet on top of the propane burner.

He stood in the sun, feeling the warmth soak into his body. Running made him feel better.

The phone kept ringing.

Depression drifted back if he missed a run.

The runs might not be a long-term solution, but they worked for now.

The tortillas were made by a woman who brought them in a beat up Chrysler all the way from Mammoth. She brought the tortillas along with selections of inlaid jewelry to town a couple times every week. Edison could smell mesquite from the fire when she handed him the foil wrapped tortillas. Edison would look at the pendants, bracelets and earrings she spread on a black velvet cloth. Inlaid cardinals, butterflies and firebirds. The woman reminded Edison of his older brother Livingston's wife Tasha, and the years they all lived in the little house on Florida Street. Livingston and Tasha took Edison and Duane in after their parents were killed.

Livingston was a surrogate father to Edison. He'd taught Edison more than how to ride and to rope. Livingston turned Edison into a genuine Indian cowboy.

The bad things happened while Edison was back east. Edison blamed himself for not being there for Livingston. He could have gone to college in-state and played football. In his darker hours, Edison blamed himself for Livingston's death.

He looked around the trailer. The 1957 Airstream Wanderer was clean and starkly appointed. Spartan. He'd bought it from an old-timer in Snowflake and brought it to Globe a couple of months ago. He'd stripped all the fussy little geegaws the man had accumulated in the trailer and outfitted it with a table and two chairs. He placed cushions on the floor and made simple shelving to accommodate his books.

He let the telephone ring. Eventually, it would stop.

The temperature was still reasonable. The blazing heat would arrive when the sun reached it's peak.

Edison looked forward to working on his current project. He'd reached a tricky part and he could use the time. In back of the trailer, Edison had constructed a lean-to shack. Inside Edison was hammering conchas out of Mexican silver pesos. He needed twelve disks and a buckle for the belt. It was a tricky process. It required uninterrupted time. He'd made sketches of a First Phase Dine' belt at the Heard Museum. He didn't want it to look *exactly* like the one at the Heard, but close. The sale of the belt would be handled in Tucson.

Edison had pared his belongings down to the essentials of food, shelter, water. Books. He had hidden away a little money in the Airstream. The hiding place was a welded pocket of the same anodized aluminum as the trailer. It wasn't a lot of money, but it was enough for emergencies.

He didn't need much. He hadn't lived in Globe

long before the mine closed. Not long enough to feel at home. Edison had grown up in Holbrook, about four hours north of Globe.

He looked at the position of the sun in the sky. It was past time to light the fire.

He grabbed a clean white T-shirt and pulled it on over his head. Edison was a powerful man. His skills as a defensive back had taken him all the way across the country to play at Dartmouth. On the field he'd been known for his vicious mid-field hits.

He had a picture from those days, leveling a wide receiver.

Sports Illustrated's college preview:
Big Hit from the Big Green.

The picture was taken before a freak play ruined his knee and ended his football career. Taken before the fight on a rainy night in Hanover when he'd left a man half dead on the street.

Edison remembered that night like a bad dream.

❊ ❊ ❊

The phone rang again. Edison stepped back toward the Wanderer, passing the pile of sawed pine he used in the kiln. He would answer the phone call, then light the fire.

Edison touched the sweaty green bandanna wrapped around his head and felt the line of salt on the cloth.

Picking up the beige phone receiver from the top of the trailer's turquoise Formica counter, Edison held it away from his ear for second or two. Whoever was calling could wait for a moment. He didn't want to let go of the peace he felt. Outside the window he saw a hawk circling. Edison glanced at the Winchester 1892 above the door of the trailer. Some kind of animal was out there wounded or dead. Maybe he should go out and put the animal out of its pain. The bird was making a second, larger circle.

"Edison?"

Edison recognized Dallas's voice.

The bird would soon make it's dive. Watching the bird circle was more interesting than listening to Dallas King. The hawk, even with it's enormous wingspan was not as big as condors Edison had seen in the Salt River Canyon.

Dallas King was on the line. Calling from his motel in Holbrook.

The Sunset Motel.

Edison had found his brother Livingston's dead body at the Sunset Motel.

Edison pictured Dallas. Dallas was a big white guy who wore guayaberra shirts. Dallas had fixed up some of the Sunset. Painted it, put in some plumbing.

Dallas had spent a lot of money on the Sunset. He'd replaced carpets, sinks, and toilets in some of the units. Nobody knew where Dallas found the money but he'd paid for everything with cash. He had renovated the units closest to the office and left the last rooms untouched. He rented the units by the hour, day, or week. Dallas's renting policy was simple. Cash only. No IOUs. You want a loan, go to the bank.

There was a sign on his desk: *In God We Trust - All Others Pay Cash.*

Livingston had lived in one of the end units.

Dallas collected rent and counted it in the office of the Sunset. No questions were asked of the tenants. No amenities were offered. The end units were wrecks of plywood, stucco and despair. Edison pictured Dallas at the plate glass window of the Sunset's office staring at women tourists who sometimes stayed at the motel.

Dallas liked standing in front of the out-sized window, his hands making marks on the glass, watching the traffic on Route 66.

Edison didn't want to talk to Dallas.

"Can't talk to you, Dallas. I'm busy."

"Edison," Dallas said. "Edison, listen just a minute. What's a *minute* hurt you?"

Dallas was trying to sound reasonable. He was trying to keep Edison on the phone.

"Can't talk," Edison said. "I'm busy."

"Edison, this is important," Dallas said.

"Told you I can't talk. I'll call you back."

"It's about a rodeo, Edison."

"Said I'd call you back."

"Come on, Edison. Just listen to what I'm saying."

Edison hung up the phone then looked at it.

Dallas would call again and again until Edison talked to him.

Edison grabbed the burro and ate it. It wasn't enough. He would get something more at Jane's Cafe in town.

✻ ✻ ✻

What the hell? Where was the schedule? Edison looked under some books.

He found the schedule under the copy of *Black Elk Speaks* he'd taken from Livingston's room at the Sunset Motel. Red letters marked Navajo Nation events. In small print were estimated jackpot amounts. This weekend there was a rodeo scheduled up in Indian Wells.

That's why Dallas was calling.

Maybe he *would* call Dallas later, after giving him a chance to stew. Dallas's number was somewhere. He could call directory assistance and ask for the Sunset Motel in Holbrook.

He looked at the belt. Edison wanted to finish it. He looked out the door at the pile of wood. If he was going to town, he wouldn't light the fire. The kiln wasn't efficient. Edison liked the feeling the heat gave and the look of the flames in the clear sky, but he wouldn't leave it unattended.

He blamed Dallas for getting sidetracked. Even though he had no deadline, Edison hated a half-finished project. The guy in Tucson would turn it into money when it was done.

Edison didn't need Dallas. He could work when he wanted. Eventually, the mine would reopen. He didn't need money.

What did he need Dallas for?

MIRACLE MILE

Locaster looked at Wanda.

She was watching *Beverly Hillbillies*, sitting with her feet propped up on the wooden desk in the motel. The motel on Tucson's Miracle Mile was quiet. The pool was closed and the neon sign was broken. Locaster was sure nobody had seen them check in or go out. Wanda looked like she didn't have a care in the world. It didn't matter if anyone saw her go out. She looked different away from the strip club.

She looked good. Short cut-off denim shorts and a Blondie T-shirt. No wonder surfer boy couldn't keep his eyes off her. Surfer boy couldn't keep his eyes *or* his hands off her. The funny thing was, Dallas thought Locaster didn't know.

Locaster knew Dallas King was a chump. Dallas believed Wanda's declarations of love.

It wasn't funny. It was human nature. Dallas believed what he *wanted* to believe. Right now. Dallas believed Wanda wanted to leave Locaster for him.

"You did a good job, Wanda, I gotta tell you."

She looked at Locaster.

"He's ready then?"

"More or less," Locaster said.

He looked at the television. Wanda looked like a sly Elly Mae Clampett.

"Why do you watch things like that?"

She had turned the television's volume down to listen to Locaster talking to Dallas.

"I'm not watching," Wanda said. "I was waiting for you to get off the phone. Did he tell you anything more?"

"Not our surfer boy. He's too careful. I'm telling you though, you did a good job."

Wanda stood up. She picked up the little makeup case she took everywhere. There were two stickers on the outside. One said *THE THING? Mystery of the Desert,* the other one was from the Carlsbad Caverns in New Mexico.

Jed and Granny were talking about something. Jed had his shotgun in the crook of his arm, but he didn't look angry. That was the thing about Jed. Locaster thought it was funny to see someone walking around with a shotgun for no reason.

Wanda snapped the television off. The set was so old the picture reduced to a white dot on the screen before disappearing.

Locaster packed his things in his Samsonite suitcase. The one he liked to brag about.

"You drop this off the bridge in Lake Havasu and it won't open," he liked to say. "Put it in a cage with a gorilla then dust it off. The suitcase is gonna be good as new. Maybe a few nicks and scratches, but it'll maintain its *structural integrity*."

Part of the case was lined in foam and Locaster kept his .357 Cobra in there with an extra box of hollow points.

"Damn thing's as versatile as hell," he had said. "You fire .38s in it then you can go back to your .357s. Can't do it the other way around."

Lotta people didn't know their calibers, Locaster always said. This could cause waste and unnecessary time. He had taken time to explain this to Wanda. She had asked questions and seemed to understand. Locaster had taken her out a few times to shoot. She showed a natural aptitude.

He packed light. Two leisure suits and a change of underwear. Locaster was an advocate of bathroom sink laundry. Wanda insisted on going to laundromats, which Locaster considered an unnecessary risk. Since the strip club job, he had stayed mostly inside.

The Samsonite was big enough for the Cobra and his clothes.

He liked his suits. They were easy to spot clean and didn't make him sweat.

"Light blue and beige," he liked to say. "Good colors for the Southwest."

He'd gotten the two shotguns in Benson, Arizona. Never used, the guy said. Untraceable, the guy assured Locaster.

He kept the shotguns in a tweed Fender case he'd bought at the Chicago Store on Congress Street in downtown Tucson. They fit nicely.

COLD PIZZA AT THE SUNSET MOTEL

Standing behind the desk at the Sunset Motel, Dallas King hung up the phone.

He resisted the urge to slam the phone down. He pulled last night's pizza out of the fridge.

What the hell was Edison's problem, anyway?

Dallas opened the box and pulled one of the slices up from the cardboard. Thought about warming it up. The pizza hadn't been great coming out of the oven. It didn't look any better this morning.

Dallas knew it was just a question of calling Edison back at the right time.

Stalling was typical of Edison. You had to court him, practically, even though you were the one doing him a favor.

The meat on the pizza looked okay. Cheese was hard. The whole thing was cold.

Edison would come around. He just needed a

little coaxing.

There were two more slices of the pizza in the box. Dallas chewed the first bite. The crust was hard, too. He decided to throw the rest of the pizza away. He'd get something to eat before everything started happening. Maybe a steak. He looked across the street at the steak house. It wouldn't open for a while. And anyway, he didn't want a steak. What he wanted was an enchilada.

Edison, Dallas could coax.

❋ ❋ ❋

Dallas thought about the earlier call from Locaster. How did Locaster manage to sound threatening, even when Dallas was holding all the cards?

Dallas dreaded seeing Locaster, but Wanda made the deal worthwhile.

Finally, she could leave Locaster. This was the only way Dallas could make it happen. Locaster's temper would make leaving him any other way dangerous for Wanda.

The plan was working. Locaster and Wanda were coming to Holbrook.

Wanda wouldn't have told Locaster the other part of the plan.

The secret part.

The part Dallas and Wanda talked about in furtive, late-night conversations.

The trap.

※ ※ ※

Dallas looked at the strip of pictures he'd scotch-taped under the glass covering his desk.

He had pushed the phone slightly while talking to Edison. Most of the time he kept the phone over the picture to keep the exposures from fading and also to avoid embarrassing questions.

The black and white shots had been taken at a coin-operated photo booth at Walgreens on the corner of 1st and Grant in Tucson.

Dallas remembered the place. The Walgreens smelled like Cheeze-It crackers. He'd waited forever for Wanda to come out of the booth. He had wondered why she didn't want Dallas to come into the booth. He had been naive back then. She had been afraid of James Locaster.

She had kept one of the strips and given Dallas this one which he'd saved as a combination souvenir and trophy. In the strip of pictures, she had made a variety of faces from silly to sultry.

Wanda Locaster was as blonde as Marilyn Monroe. She took Dallas's breath away. He looked at Wanda's pictures again. Remembered the night she took the pictures. Their one night together in Tucson.

He remembered the place but not the name.

The motel sign was a sleeping Mexican, under an enormous sombrero.

La Siesta? El Sombrero?

❊ ❊ ❊

He slid the phone back over the black and white photographs and tried to contain his anger. Dallas needed Edison to come up here to Holbrook.

He needed to approach Edison the right way. Dallas knew Edison had family problems which were affecting him.

Dallas understood family problems. Dallas had been born with them.

❊ ❊ ❊

Dallas King and Tony King had the same grandfather. The old man had owned both the Ten High Saloon and a pawn shop during Holbrook's wild years.

A rumor around town said their grandfather had paid for both with gold from an army payroll robbery.

The grandfather had lugged the gold into town in two valises, bought the saloon and the pawn shop, then died with the remainder hidden away.

The rumor had turned into legend by the time either Tony or Dallas heard of it.

* * *

After high school, Dallas had intended to leave Holbrook for Los Angeles. Tony's side of the family retained the pawn shop and sold the saloon. Dallas's family inherited nothing.

Dallas couldn't wait to leave Holbrook. He hoped to meet Dick Dale in Los Angeles. Dallas wanted to join Dale's surf band. He'd packed his clothes in his suitcase, carefully folding the specially matched blue plaid blazer and pants outfit from Sears. With his white turtleneck and his mod sideburns, Dallas had been told he bore more than a slight resemblance to Glen Campbell.

Dallas intended to go directly to Los Angeles via the Greyhound Bus Line. Between Holbrook and Winslow, however, Dallas met James Locaster.

Locaster explained to Dallas he was traveling to Tucson by way of Flagstaff, describing his job as management for a regional entertainment operation.

Locaster would be reuniting with his wife Wanda in Tucson,

James Locaster recognized in Dallas an eagerness to make something of himself. Locaster urged Dallas to exchange his ticket for the more flexible Ameripass and join him in traveling south to Tucson.

Locaster had a worn brochure for the program in his attache. Smiling Ameripass passengers stood in front of the Statue of Liberty in one picture and St. Louis's Gateway Arch in the next.

"Los Angeles can wait, Dallas," Locaster said.

He held the brochure under Dallas's nose.

"You get one of these passes in Flagstaff, you got your own private coach wherever you want to go. Los Angeles will always be there. It's always gonna be there less you get an earthquake."

He winked.

Locaster was always winking.

The pass offered unlimited mileage wherever Greyhound traveled. Coincidentally, Greyhound traveled to all of Locaster's stops.

"Saves me a ton of money on expenses," Locaster said.

Winking.

"And what the IRS don't know won't hurt them."

Both Locaster and Dallas laughed. As if Locaster was paying the IRS.

Their first business meeting was held at Gordo's Mexicateria way out on Broadway in Tucson.

Locaster's wife had joined them.

Wanda Locaster.

She looked about twenty years old. James had to be over fifty.

Locaster kept a package of Tiparillos next to the sleeve of his beige leisure suit. He lighted one of the long, slender cigars and the waitress dropped an orange plastic ashtray next to him.

The smoke made her wrinkle her nose slightly while she passed out the plastic menus.

Gordo's, according to the Locaster was famous for chimichangas. The real deal, though, was their all-you-can-eat option.

"Just raise that little flag there," Locaster said. "They bring you more of whatever you want.

Locaster and Dallas both ordered all-you-can-eat.

Wanda, after some deliberation, tossed the menu down.

"I'll have that diet plate," she said.

Locaster winked at Dallas.

"She'll be bugging me for some guacamole. You just wait and see."

Dallas hadn't been sure who would be picking up the tab, but he would have been happy to pay for Wanda's cottage cheese and pear. For the rest of her life, maybe. Locaster could pay for his own.

Dallas figured Wanda was trapped with James Locaster.

She was waiting to be released from bondage by someone wearing a mix-and-match baby blue plaid suit from Sears.

By Dallas.

Locaster was an expert in both the Tilt-a-Whirl and the Boppin' Berries carnival rides. When he explained the rides, he might as well have been explaining the monetary system of Outer Mongolia. Dallas was more interested in Wanda.

"You get right down to it, you're just a mechanic

for these damn things. They're always breaking down. You want to learn it, though, I'll teach you."

He looked at Dallas, appraising the younger man's face.

Dallas, seeing some reaction was required, snorted and pushed his hands away dismissively.

"Man," he said, "damn thing got a flywheel, I can fix it."

Locaster nodded.

❊ ❊ ❊

Locaster taught Dallas how to operate the carnival rides, and a whole lot more.

Dallas soon figured out Locaster was involved in a lot more than operating the Tilt-a-Whirl. Locaster kept dropping hints, telling Dallas he had a way to make a whole lot more money than they made operating afternoon thrill rides. And Locaster always had more money than he could have made in the carnival trade.

Later, Dallas realized Locaster had been testing him, seeing if he could trust Dallas.

When Locaster proposed the first armed robbery, Dallas was only mildly surprised. Locaster's plan was compelling and low risk.

And Wanda would be a part of it too.

The three of them would be a team.

❊ ❊ ❊

During the two years Dallas spent with Locaster and Wanda, the three of them robbed banks, Circle K's, even a funeral home.

Carnival work was only seasonal for Locaster.

In the last robbery of a Tucson strip club, the three took away an unexpected haul of money from a drug deal which had been taking place in the back room.

Wanda had started to dance at the Crawl-Back-Inn on Speedway Boulevard, 'the ugliest street in America.' With her girl-next-door looks, it was easy for her to get work there.

Locaster didn't mind Wanda stripping for an audience.

"She's very talented," he said. "Plus, it's business. She knows what to look for in these places. You never know what's going in and out of them."

Wanda kept her eyes and ears open and found out when the most money was going through the place.

The place was rolling in cash twice a month after Air Force paydays at Davis Monthan.

She didn't know about the dope money the bikers were running through the back.

The extra cash was an unexpected bonus.

Locaster didn't make any effort to explain it to Dallas. The Locasters and Dallas were living in a trailer court near the Crawl-Back-Inn.

Dallas was working on Wanda, trying to convince her to leave Locaster and run away with him.

Just a couple more jobs, she kept saying. Locaster was a genius for planning, and they always needed more money.

Also, she told Dallas about Locaster's violent streak. She would have already left him, if she could have. Wanda was afraid of him.

Because of Wanda, they knew exactly when to hit the Crawl-Back-Inn and where to stand with the shotguns.

They didn't need to fire a shot.

They never needed to during the whole time Dallas worked with Locaster and Wanda.

Locaster said only amateurs fired their weapons indiscriminately. If the operations were properly planned, gunfire was rarely needed.

"That's the movies, Dallas," Locaster said.

People only fired if things were going wrong.

Dallas thought about the way Wanda looked the one night they had spent together. He remembered the way she lay on the bed in the darkened motel, neon light from the window playing on her sleeping face.

Locaster had arranged for them to meet later, after the three had separated following the Crawl-Back-Inn.

Wanda had made a head signal to Dallas and handed him a pack of matches. On the back she had written the address of the motel on Miracle Mile and the time when Dallas could meet her.

Their only time together.

He asked her if she would marry him when she got away from Locaster.

Wanda just looked at him.

"Dallas, we're as much as married right now. You want paperwork, that's just gonna have to wait. It's just a question of when we can be together."

Dallas had nodded.

They were as good as married.

She'd left late, telling Dallas Locaster would be suspicious if she didn't get back with him at the pre-arranged time.

She said she'd find a way to get Locaster to bring her to Holbrook, but before she did, Dallas came up with the plan.

It looked like it would work.

ANTONIO'S REVENGE

Behind the counter of King's Pawn and Trade, Tony King was taking apart a little two shot derringer he'd bought from a guy the hour before. Fiddling with the thing, really. He took off the gray sunglasses he usually wore, replacing them with magnifiers in order to take the little bitch apart. Tony King had more than a hundred weapons in his personal arsenal. A lot more than a hundred, but Tony didn't like people knowing his personal business so he didn't keep them out where they could be seen. He needed weapons to protect his small empire of old coins, dead pawn, and liquor. You never knew when some hot rod might come in all hopped up and try to hold up the place. Tony would be ready. Nobody would dare to try getting past Tony King. He almost wished they would.

He picked up the phone and dialed the numbers.

"How you doing, Dallas. How's the Big D?"

Tony pictured his cousin. Big and dumb. Dallas had just gotten the tattoo. *Big D*. Like anybody was going to call Dallas '*Big D*'.

"Tony, you calling me about tonight?"

"What else am I calling you for, Dallas? What the hell's wrong with you?"

"Tony, you gotta lay off, man."

"Right," Tony said. "I'm gonna lay off. We make a deal and I'll lay off."

Dallas said nothing.

Tony waited. His cousin Dallas was some kind of genius, right? It took forever for a simple thought to get through his thick blonde skull. Dallas was like the big concrete dinosaurs down the street from the pawn shop. Dallas was as dumb as one of those.

"You think about it? I know what you got, Dallas. I know how you got it. Bring some cash, Dallas. Then we can talk."

Tony smiled. This was where he would make Dallas sweat. He'd done it since they were kids.

"I know how you got it."

Those were the magic words.

Dumb as he was, Dallas had stumbled onto some money.

Tony wanted some. It was only fair.

"I thought about it, Tony," Dallas said.

"What's your answer?"

"You gonna be up at your place around eight tonight?"

"What are you talking about? I'm always here."

"Okay Tony. Eight o'clock."

Dallas was dumb as one of the chunks of petrified wood Tony sold.

He probably figured he could pay Tony off.

"Eight o'clock, Dallas. Don't be late."

Tony hung up the phone and looked down at the derringer.

At least an hour had passed, but Tony was still thinking about the man who had come into the pawn shop.

In the parking lot, a station wagon had pulled in from the highway.

The man had gotten out of the car.

He had his wife and kids in the car and household goods packed in the back. With Indiana plates, they were probably heading west. The man walked into the pawn shop.

He came up to the counter and told Tony he had a gun he wanted to sell.

"I got it in my pocket," the man said. "I just need some gas money."

The man might have been forty. He looked like some kind of down-on-his-luck professor. Thin, balding, wire glasses and dirty white shirt.

"Bring it out slow, with two fingers, partner," Tony said.

At least the guy had the smarts to tell him he had a gun. If he'd come in holding the little pea shooter, Tony might have shot him.

Fortunately for the guy, he had a grain of sense.

The pearl handled derringer was cute, and Tony said so. Twin barrels, over and under. You could put a shotgun shell in the top and a load for business on the bottom. Either one would do the job from less than four feet. A belly gun. Something for just in case. Hardly worth Tony's time.

Tony looked out at the car. The man's wife and the kids were moving around in there.

Tony pulled open the cash register and took out a twenty and a ten.

"I'm being generous here," Tony said. "You can take it or leave it. You don't want to run out of gas. Not when you're heading into the heat." Tony looked at the derringer again. "You shouldn't have something like this around children, anyway. It ain't no cap gun."

The man gave Tony a look, but reached for the bills.

"Do I need to sign anything?"

Tony smirked. Waved his hand away from the man. "Got it all taken care of at this end. Nothing to sign, partner."

Tony looked out at the car again. One of the kids, a little boy, had his face pushed up to the window. Tony pulled a bag of potato chips off the rack in back of him.

Hesitated, then took down another bag.

Chee-tos. Kids liked them.

"Go ahead now. I'm throwing these in."

The man took the chips and the money and headed toward the door.

"Gas is out by the highway," Tony said. "That'll get you to California, maybe."

The last Tony had seen, gas was priced at fifty seven cents. He laughed. They could get some dip to go with the chips, maybe a bag of Kool-aid and make it a party.

The pearl handled derringer *was* cute. It could kill someone or blow up in your hand. Tony took it apart and cleaned it before winding a white tag around the baby sized hammer.

He figured he'd make a profit on it, one way or another.

❋ ❋ ❋

Tony started with a big rock as a kid. Ten or eleven years old. Watching a wino sleeping off a drunk outside the Bucket of Blood Saloon, Tony decided to have a little fun. There were plenty of rocks outside his family's pawn shop. Some of them were in barrels and were marked for sale. Those were the petrified wood shards, and then there were the black pieces of obsidian which looked like chunks of glass. Those were also for sale. Tony knew not to grab any of those rocks. He could get in trouble throwing *them*.

There were plenty of other rocks down by the railroad tracks. Near the Bucket of Blood there were even more.

Tony picked out some good sized ones. Ones he knew he could chuck like a big-leaguer. He carried a big rock in one hand and put a couple more in his jeans pockets. He scooped up some loose pebbles and carried them in his other hand. Shrapnel. Running as close as he dared, Tony pitched the first rock then retreated into the shadows to watch.

Watching the reaction was the best part. Tony wasn't trying to injure the guy. He remembered laughing, watching the man sit up and hold his head. The guy looked around to see what had happened. He had watched the man get up unsteadily and then fall down again. The man puked, which made Tony laugh again. While the man was on his hands and knees, Tony released the shrapnel. The small pebbles pelted the man who then slipped onto his face.

Tony couldn't wait to do it again.

He only did it once more.

He'd used the same procedure the next time. First he threw the big rock to wake the wino up. Except the first rock didn't awaken him. It took a second rock, thrown into the man's ribs to elicit a groan. Then Tony let loose with the shrapnel. It was as hilarious as the first time. Tony was really having a good time until he felt himself being picked up by the back of his sweatshirt and his belt.

Deputy Sheriff Lot Conover held him up over the street, then carried him to the railroad track. Tony was big for his age, but Conover held him like a feather pillow.

Conover was big and as strong as hell.

The deputy turned Tony around and spoke to him. Tony never forgot the look in Conover's eyes or the sound of the crossing bell.

Conover held Tony next to the passing train.

Inches away from the thundering freight cars.

Tony couldn't hear everything Conover said. Most of the deputy's words were drowned out by the Santa Fe freight train.

But he got the message. Conover knew Tony's family and knew turning Tony over to them would be useless. Conover would take care of Tony himself if he caught him again.

Conover had called him by his real name.

"Antonio," Conover said.

They could both feel the train rumble.

"Antonio," Conover said, "this train comes by every day. You need to stay away from it."

Tony had been frightened, but his fear turned into something else. He worked out imaginary revenge strategies. Not just revenge against Conover. Tony also blamed the wino. If the guy hadn't been sleeping off his drunk there, Tony never would have run into Conover.

And he wouldn't have kept seeing Conover and the train in his dreams.

❊ ❊ ❊

Tony moved on to knives. Working at the family pawn shop, Tony became an expert in the various blades. He never went anywhere without at least a switchblade strapped to his ankle. Tony acquired a collection of knives and later firearms. He still dreamed about revenge on Conover, but didn't dare take action. Everyone knew about Conover's expertise with guns. Tony wouldn't have dared challenge Conover.

Tony thought about Dallas. His cousin knew Tony's temper. Dallas knew from experience not to mess with Tony.

The thing bothering Tony was Dallas's money. Where had his cousin gotten the cash to buy and fix up the motel?

Dallas didn't work, but he had plenty of cash.

He hadn't earned it as a carny.

Tony laughed. Maybe Dallas *had* finally found the gold.

They'd looked for it together as kids. They'd even used a Ouija board to try finding it.

They would have split it, fifty-fifty if they ever found it.

Dallas had found *something*. Tony was sure of it. And whatever Dallas had, he was going to share.

Fifty-fifty.

❄ ❄ ❄

Tony put the derringer back together. Snapped the hinge mechanism. It was as simple a little killing machine as had ever been invented. Effective, but unreliable. You slap one of these down on a table, you better be sure it was pointing away from you. Tony unlocked the glass cabinet in front of the phone. Placed the derringer on the black velvet with which he'd lined the shelf. Ready for sale. He laughed. Literally a Saturday night special.

What the hell, he thought. He dug around behind the counter. Found a .410 shell and a .45 cartridge. They both fit in the gun, slicker than snot.

He rolled his right-hand jean leg up.

The derringer fit snug inside his boot.

JOHNNY ANGEL KNOCKED HIM OUT

Locaster and Wanda would drive up from Tucson, so it would take at least six hours. Probably more when you factored in the time Locaster would take getting out of the car and stretching.

Somewhere around Globe they'd get something to eat or else they would be out of luck until Show Low.

So it would be a while. Fine with Dallas. He could use the extra time setting things up just right.

Dallas could picture Locaster and Wanda on their drive up through Catalina, Mammoth, Winkelman.

❋ ❋ ❋

Right now, Locaster and Wanda would be

winding down into the Salt River Canyon. Locaster would be yakking away and Wanda would be forced to listen to him.

Unless she had that look in her eye where you wondered if she was really there or not.

One more time, Dallas wondered why Locaster had gone back to Tucson.

It didn't sound like Locaster. Going back to where the bikers who ran the strip joint on Speedway could find him.

Locaster was smarter than that.

But it didn't pay to question Locaster's plans. Locaster generally was right. But also, you didn't want to listen to him explaining *why* he was right.

❊ ❊ ❊

Dallas remembered Locaster describing his family ancestry that first night at Gordo's Mexicateria.

Locaster said he was the descendant of a Norman knight who accompanied William the Conqueror at the Battle of Hastings. Something like eighteen great-grandfathers back.

"They were like *this*, man. They were *tight*."

James held up his thumb and forefinger to show the the relationship between the king and the knight.

"William woulda done anything for my great-great-great, and my great-great-great woulda done anything for William."

It was late at night and Gordo's Mexicateria was about to close. The waitress was clearing their table and giving Locaster a dirty look.

They were almost the last patrons left. At another table, a fat man was finishing up.

The guy walked to their booth and asked Locaster for a smoke.

Locaster had grabbed his Tiparillos and put them in his shirt pocket.

There was nobody else there except Wanda and Dallas.

Wanda gave the guy a cigarette, and even lighted a match for him.

"Thanks," the guy said, looking at Wanda. He turned and glowered at Locaster.

Everybody loved Wanda. Pretty much came with the territory.

Dallas had his eye on Wanda.

She wasn't listening to Locaster.

She wore a Frampton Comes Alive T-shirt, her white-rimmed sunglasses were propped on top of her head, and she had a look on her face. The one Dallas would get to know better later. At the time, he thought she was stoned.

Wanda was *much* younger than Locaster.

She reminded Dallas of one of those beach movie actresses.

Ride the Wild Surf was his favorite.

Wanda looked bored. Whatever Locaster and Dallas were saying didn't interest her.

At first Dallas thought Wanda was Locaster's

daughter.

Wanda pulled a cigarette out of a beaded leather pouch. A Virginia Slim. She lighted it and pulled the orange ashtray close to her.

"You look like one of those surfer boys they got out in California," Locaster said. "You know what I'm talking about? Like Jan and Dean, those guys. You go into a place, all the girls gonna be looking at is you. Men gonna be looking at Wanda, if you go in together. Am I right?"

Wanda looked at Dallas. Dallas looked at her.

She left a ring of cherry red lipstick on the filter of the Virginia Slim.

Shelley Fabares and Barbara Eden were both in Ride the Wild Surf.

Dallas felt Shelley Fabares was very underrated. *Johnny Angel* knocked him out.

Wanda rolled her eyes and looked out toward the parking lot and the palm tree standing next to Broadway.

Dallas was head over heels from then on.

It didn't make a damn bit of difference to him she was married to Locaster.

If the two of them *were* married.

Either way, it didn't make any difference to Dallas. Locaster was too old for her.

Locaster thought Dallas would fit in well with his business.

Dallas's bland good looks were perfect, he said.

※ ※ ※

Locaster and Wanda hadn't gotten to Holbrook yet.

Dallas went to the back of the office of the Sunset Motel. It was time to find the prescription bottle.

In the bathroom, he opened the medicine cabinet. He had a collection of bandages, a bottle of iodine, an Ace bandage, white tape, a set of tiny screwdrivers for repairing the wings of a pair of glasses, nail clippers, and a postcard from Socorro, New Mexico signed by Wanda.

He pushed all the detritus to the side and found the bottle he was looking for.

He'd bought it just in case on an afternoon foray into Nogales, Sonora.

Old Mexico, Locaster called it.

Locaster had taken Dallas and Wanda down there after their first heist.

Three years ago, Dallas thought.

Locaster and Wanda had been waiting in the restaurant for the shrimp to be brought out.

Locaster was talking about the Germans who had come to Mexico and started brewing beer and raising hell with their automatic weaponry. Locaster was half in the bag, which was a little unusual.

Dallas had slipped out of the cantina while Locaster was explaining something about the difference between German and English grammar.

He went into the little *Farmacia* next to the restaurant. The shelves in the dimly lit place were lined with bottles of vanilla, coffee liqueur, and high proof grain alcohol.

Dallas thought he would need to wake the druggist up from a late afternoon siesta but the man was only reclining.

At first the druggist pretended not to know what Dallas was asking for.

Dallas couldn't remember what it was called. Chloral something.

He'd pantomimed using an eyedropper and putting something into a drink.

Made like he was falling asleep.

Like he was playing charades. First word. Sounds like…

The druggist scowled. Shook his finger. No, no, no.

No dropper. He brought a bottle with four pills. Made a cutting motion.

Dallas nodded. Cut one in half.

The druggist smiled and closed his eyes briefly. Faked a snore.

Dallas pointed at the bottle. Held up four fingers.

"What happens you take all four?"

The druggist scowled again. Shook his head vehemently and waggled his finger.

"No, no, no."

The druggist crossed his hands over his chest,

closed his eyes and pushed out a gray tongue.

"*Santa Muerte*," the druggist said.

Dallas nodded, then pulled his wallet out, hoping his absence hadn't been noticed upstairs at the restaurant.

He pulled out an American bill. Raised his eyebrows.

The druggist quickly shook his head. Held up two fingers. Pointed at the bill.

Dallas looked over both his shoulders and pulled out another bill.

The druggist smiled and pushed his hands forward as if to scoot Dallas toward the door.

Locaster looked up at Dallas, coming back to the table.

"Usually Montezuma's revenge comes after eating."

Dallas had felt himself blush and touched the little bottle he had put into his jacket pocket.

He'd heard about these.

A Mickey Finn. He wasn't sure when he'd need one, but figured he was here in Mexico, why not?

He didn't need any pinata, or anything else they were selling.

❈ ❈ ❈

The plan was coming together.

There were a lot of moving parts. Like the Tilt-a-Whirl.

Even though the Tilt-a-Whirl went around in

a random, chaotic pattern, the same number of riders started as the ones who finished.

Locaster loved talking about the mechanics of the Tilt-a-Whirl like he was some kind of physicist.

Dallas thought about the plan and the schedule. It wouldn't be easy, but he knew he could do it.

He and Wanda could do it.

SWEAT-STAINED GUAYABERRA

Driving his Ford pickup to Jane's Cafe, Edison tried thinking of some reasons why he couldn't rodeo this weekend. He didn't really have anything against Dallas. Nothing tangible, anyway.

Dallas kept calling. Dallas would try to get Edison to compete in Indian Wells.

Claiming he was too busy making the belt was not a good excuse.

❋ ❋ ❋

Edison barely knew Dallas before Dallas came back from wherever the hell he'd been and bought the motel.

Dallas was older than Edison by several years. There was no reason they should have known one another.

Edison never recalled seeing him until around the time Livingston started going downhill. By that time, Livingston had moved part time into the

Sunset Motel.

Livingston's wife hated Dallas.

"Your brother pays good money to that scuzzball to live in there," Tasha said. "There's no reason why he needs to stay there. No reason at all."

❊ ❊ ❊

Dallas made a point of meeting Edison after Livingston died.

Edison remembered Dallas pushing into the booth at the El Rey Cafe a few days after Livingston was killed. Edison had been eating lunch.

Dallas told Edison he owned the Sunset Motel. He was trying to be friendly, asking Edison if he still did any rodeos.

Edison regretted telling Dallas he wanted to rodeo again.

Dallas told Edison he had traveled all around the southwest in the mobile entertainment business.

Edison figured out Dallas had been a carny.

Dallas even made a pitch for Edison to join the carnival.

"I don't deny the business gets a bad rap," Dallas said. "But it's good money, Edison. I could get you on. Before too long, you could own your own outfit, a smart guy like you. It's more than you'll ever make with your fancy degree. Plus, you get to meet ladies. They drop off the kids when they shop for groceries and when they come back there you are. Right? It's like shooting fish in a barrel."

※ ※ ※

Edison remembered Dallas pitching the carnival in his sweat-stained guayaberra.

Acting like he was offering Edison a job with a Fortune 500 corporation.

Fish in a damn barrel.

※ ※ ※

Edison couldn't think of any good reason why he couldn't ride this weekend.

Dallas wouldn't even be at the rodeo.

Dallas set things up, but he wouldn't get his own hands dirty.

Dallas would make his money, though.

And Edison wanted to compete.

Dallas would make some money betting. He'd pass some on to Edison.

What the hell?

Why not?

LEGENDS OF THE WEST

Whatever Dallas was hiding was no small amount of money.

Tony was determined to figure it out. With his contacts around the state and in New Mexico, it probably wouldn't take him long. Tony didn't care what Dallas was into as long as he cooperated.

So far, Dallas was cooperating. Probably shaking like a leaf, but he was cooperating.

Tony grabbed a bag of potato chips from the rack.

Opened it and spread the chips out on the counter.

If he could get Merlinda Beach to work here, she could go out back and make him a sandwich or something.

Merlinda Beach. Probably still living in Holbrook so she could keep her eye on her half-crazy grandfather up on the rez.

He wasn't sure he wanted her at the pawn shop full time, but there would be some advantages.

The radio was playing something by Ronnie

Milsap.

He wasn't sure he could completely trust Merlinda .

Tony liked to think he treated people fairly, but some people had an inflated opinion of the worth of their valuables.

Tony looked around the pawn shop. Radios, guitars, power saws. Glass cases filled with dead pawn. It took money to keep this place up. You couldn't just let cash walk out the door. Merlinda was getting to be a situation. He was going to have to decide what he wanted to do about her. In the meantime, he didn't want her getting any ideas. Like saying she was done with him. What the hell did she mean by that? Who did she think she was she could call the shots?

Tony looked down at the derringer. He could get sixty, maybe seventy bucks for it, depending who was interested. It might be a collector's item. Maybe he'd go out back and fire it. Derringers kicked. There wasn't really anything on the damn thing but the barrel.

He'd tell Merlinda when he was done with her. Maybe they *were* done. But Tony would be the one doing the deciding.

Tony thought about the meeting he was going to have with Dallas. Tonight at eight. Dallas was good and scared about something. When Tony started hinting around about it, Dallas got nervous. He'd given Tony a funny look like he'd been caught doing something. Dallas was stupid. Acting like he'd made his money driving some carnival ride. Who would believe that bullshit, anyway? Dallas paid cash for the Sunset and thought he was going to make money now that the highway was running.

Nobody got off the highway to stay in Holbrook anymore.

Those days were over.

It must have cost Dallas something to buy the place and fix it up.

Dallas spending money got Tony's attention. Dallas was hiding something.

But Tony knew Dallas didn't have the guts to stand up to him.

Tony might wonder where Dallas got the cash, but really, where the money came from didn't make a damn bit of difference.

PEDAL STEEL

His name was Forrest Canyon, and he considered himself one of the best steel guitar players outside Nashville. One of the best pedal steel players no longer living in Nashville. He wasn't sure he would go back there, even if he could. There were too many hippies coming in. Anyway, Nashville wasn't the same as it had been back in the old days. Years ago Forrest Canyon had the opportunity to sit down with Ernest Tubb one night at a bar and have a couple of beers. Now it was all politics. All about who you knew. Even if old Ernest was still walking the floor, there was no way Forrest Canyon would have been able to get close to him, let alone sit down and drink beers with the man.

Those days were over. Thanks, he thought. Just like the Ernest Tubb song.

Thanks. Thanks a lot.

He'd had enough, even before the problems came and the police detective started coming around to knock on the door of the motel room he'd rented at Ye Olde Colonial and started talking to Forrest about where he'd been when such and such happened.

All right. He knew the girl. He wouldn't deny knowing her. But Forrest would have sworn on a stack of Ye Olde Colonial's Gideon Bibles he thought she was older.

This was a misunderstanding leading to a consequent accusation. He had been closed-mouth with the detectives, but Forrest felt it better to leave Nashville before he was officially escorted out.

Forrest didn't like the situation much, but shrugged it off. He wasn't a star, and never would be. He might get to wear sequins on his jacket, but they never dragged the steel guy to the center of the stage.

There was a whole pile of self-righteous hypocrisy, too. Some things were fine if you were Elvis, or even old Jerry Lee.

How old was Priscilla when Elvis started dating her?

He didn't even have to say anything about the Killer.

Living out of his car wasn't terrible. He kept his pedal steel guitar and a Fender Vibro Champ amplifier in the trunk of the Pontiac. The double necked Sho-Bud he'd gotten for next to nothing in a pawn shop in Texarkana. The whole set up was easy as pie to pull out of the trunk and set up.

He made a living from town to town.

In every bar there was always a little combo where he could sit in, slide into the chorus, make the band sound pro for at least one night. Turn a little place like the dive he'd left into the Ryman. All he had to do was play a few licks, and the band knew he was the real thing. He'd gotten a nice handful of cash in Amarillo. More than Forrest expected. He had used some of the money to buy himself a big steak with all the fixings at the place on the highway and to put more oil in the Pontiac. Filled up the tank. He might have just enough to get him to Barstow. From there he would go to Bakersfield, where he knew some guys who knew some guys.

He could get work in Bakersfield, he was sure of it.

They weren't as fussy or as uptight in Bakersfield as they were in Nashville.

Forrest wasn't the first musician who had done time.

He sure as hell wasn't going to prison again on the say-so of some lying girl.

And his stretch in prison had been a misunderstanding anyway. It didn't have anything to do with girls. It had to do with some money he'd been given for pay. Looking back on it, he should probably have smelled trouble. The cash was funny.

The feds didn't care what Forrest said about the money. They didn't care how Forrest had gotten it in pay. They didn't want to hear his side of the story. They just busted him.

What did the public defender ask Forrest?

"Why did you pass the money, if you knew it

was fake?"

"It looked good to me," Forrest had said. "I'm no expert. I'm a musician. Whattya want from me?"

❧ ❧ ❧

He needed one more gig before the big stretch of desert. Forrest remembered hearing about a place outside the town coming up. Holbrook, Arizona. First stop past Gallup, and he sure as *hell* wasn't stopping in Gallup. Holbrook sounded like the kind of place the town fathers might have named after a bank president eighty years ago. Some guy with peachy cheeks and a celluloid collar. The kind of man who hated a man like Forrest Canyon.

The name of the town didn't promise much. Not compared to places like Tombstone, Dodge City, or Leadville.

But if the joint had live music, sawdust on the floor, and served beer, Forrest could make a couple of bucks there, treat himself to a steak, and keep on going.

The Ten High.

That was the name of the joint.

It sounded like either a poker hand or cheap whiskey.

NO BETTER MEXICAN FOOD

"Edison, the phone call's for you," Jane said. "I don't mind you taking calls here, honey, but maybe your friend might be able to find a better time than this."

Jane held the receiver of the phone across the linoleum counter, looking like she'd drop it any minute. Jane was right. It was the busiest time of the day. With a pitcher of tea in her other hand, she ducked under the bridge formed by the telephone cord when Edison Graves took the receiver from her, almost pushing the sugar container off the counter. Edison caught it before it slid off.

Whatever was coming out of the kitchen smelled good to Edison. Some kind of chili relleno like the guy down the counter was eating.

"Whattya know, Edison?"

Dallas King. No surprise.

Dallas knew Edison frequently went to Jane's to eat. Edison had mentioned it to him. It seemed like Dallas knew everything about him.

"I was going to ask *you* that, Dallas."

"Big money. Big *goddamn* money," Dallas said. "Indian Wells Rodeo this weekend. *Helluva* jackpot, partner. No competition for you in bronco riding. First is yours for the taking, Edison. I got you all signed up. All you gotta do is show your face, cowboy."

Dallas. Always selling. He must have gotten it from his carny days, Edison thought. Dallas and the Tilt-a-Whirl.

Acting as if the Indian Wells Rodeo was a magnet drawing Edison to the north.

"What makes you think I'm coming up? I might have some plans, Dallas."

"You got plans?" Dallas paused. "You can just go ahead and put 'em on hold. You just get up here. Pay me back later. Maybe don't pay me back at all you make a good ride. Then it's on me. It's on the Big D, you know what I mean? Don't worry about it, anyway. I know you aren't working with the mine being shut down."

Dallas would be betting on the rodeo. He always had an angle, Livingston had said.

"Maybe I got another job, Dallas. Maybe I'm moonlighting."

There wasn't a better Mexican place in the state than Jane's.

Jane put an enormous plate of the green chili in front of Edison.

Green chili served with flour tortillas on the side.

"Hurry up with your call, Edison" she said.

"Whatever it is can wait. This chili can't."

"Who's that chiquita you're talking to, Edison?" Dallas said. "Sounds like you're getting yourself in some kind of trouble down there."

Edison unrolled the napkin from around the silverware. Tore a corner from the tortilla and dug into the chili.

Chiquita? Jane? Pictures of her grandchildren hung behind the register.

Edison looked out the cafe window at his parked truck.

He had more than three quarters of a tank of gas in the truck. He could drive through the canyon and up to Show Low.

He would stop back by the trailer and pick up his bedroll and be in Holbrook before dark.

The copper mine had been closed for weeks and there was no way to guess when it would open again.

Even if it meant dealing with Dallas, the rodeo was tempting

"You talking about Indian Wells, Dallas?"

"Just get here Friday, Edison. Meet me at the Ten High. I'll fill you in on the details."

Edison didn't say anything, just held the phone away from his ear.

"Whattya say then, Edison?" Dallas said.

Edison waited.

"Something else," Dallas said.

"Uh huh," Edison said.

"Got something else might be interesting to

you. You remember Merlinda Beach, don't you? Nice looking girl. Didn't you and her have a thing, one time? Seems like I remember that."

Edison shook his head. Touched his bandanna.

"I know Merlinda. Yeah, I know her. We were friends."

Goddamn Dallas. What the hell was he trying to pull?

"That's what I thought," Dallas said. "I remember seeing a picture of you and her. Maybe like a prom picture? Where did I see that? Maybe your brother had it? Shit, I can't remember. Anyway, she's asked me about you maybe a hundred times. So, today, I saw her and I thought, shit, I'm talking to Edison today. I said, come on up to the Ten High, Merlinda. Come on up and see him yourself."

Dallas knew what would get Edison up there.

Edison didn't say anything. Livingston had the picture in the motel room. Edison in a tuxedo and Merlinda in the prom dress.

Most likely Tasha had the picture now.

Dallas broke the silence.

"All right, Edison, I'll see you at the Ten High, right? She'll be there at seven. She wants to see you and believe me, she looks better than ever."

"How much you say the jackpot was, Dallas?"

"I never told you. You just gotta trust me on this one, Edison," Dallas said. "I'll tell you all about it at the Ten High. Listen, did you even hear me about Merlinda? She wants to see you something bad, Edison."

"You sure this was Merlinda Beach?" Edison said.

Dallas laughed.

"You coming up then?"

Goddamn Dallas.

He *always* won.

Edison gave the phone back to Jane. She took it, hung it up, turned back to Edison.

"How's your lunch?" she said.

Jane hovered above Edison. Making sure he was happy with the chili.

Edison nodded then smiled.

"Still the best in town," he said.

❋ ❋ ❋

Edison took another sip of the tea from the big red plastic cup. Crunched a piece of the ice. Jane took his plate. Put down the bill.

Edison liked this place. He came here nearly every day and Jane always signed her name at the bottom of the bill with a smiley face.

"You going up rodeoing, Edison?"

Edison adjusted his hat, pushing it back on his head. She'd been listening. He got off the stool, pulled up his jeans and pulled out his wallet.

"That's what they're telling me," he said.

"You come back in one piece, honey. Don't get yourself killed."

She leaned across the counter and patted Edison's hand.

"I mean it," she said.

Edison hoped he wasn't making a mistake. Dealing with Dallas was a two edged sword. You might make some money, but there was alway a price to pay. But then Dallas mentioned Merlinda.

Edison dropped a ten spot over the bill.

A healthy tip.

Nothing wrong with being generous.

He'd be fine.

SUNSET AND NEON

Dallas hung up the phone. Now *that* was a whole lot better. The call to Edison went just right. The part about Merlinda Beach was a stroke of genius. He needed to talk to Merlinda, though. Edison wasn't nearly as smart as he thought he was. It was important to get Edison up here by whatever means necessary.

That meant talking to Merlinda.

Dallas felt like a secret agent. He looked at his reflection in the full-length mirror he had installed in the motel office. Dallas was a regular guayaberra-wearing James Bond.

He liked being mysterious.

Like his grandfather, Dallas had shown up in Holbrook loaded with money. In the case of Dallas, it was a triumphant return to a town which had treated him like a nobody. He hadn't brought gold, but he had brought plenty of cash. Enough to buy The Sunset. Nobody in town really knew where Dallas's money came from. Dallas only had one little problem. A little problem named Tony King. Tony King had spent his life picking on Dallas. They were cousins, but not friends. Tony King had figured something out. Dallas knew it. Tony was asking too many questions. And Tony knew too many people. Dallas lived in fear Tony would ask some questions about a particular strip bar in Tucson called the Crawl-Back-Inn. Locaster had taken too much money out of that job.

Dallas remembered standing in the strip club, holding a shotgun, watching the reaction of the guys at the table. He and Locaster had the drop on them. If the bikers had reached for their guns they would have been dead. At least Locaster had the sense to keep Wanda out of that operation. The bikers would have recognized Wanda, no matter what she was wearing.

Dallas knew they had made a mistake as soon as he watched Locaster spread the cash out after the job. It was too much money.

Maybe Locaster hadn't gotten it through his thick head, but Dallas heard questions were already going around down in Tucson and the rest of the state. The bikers weren't going to write the loss off as a business expense. This was bodies-left-in-the-desert kind of money. Serious business. And Tony knew people. Tony knew people who would know about the Crawl-Back-Inn. Dallas could picture Tony finding out about the Tucson strip club and then putting two and two together. Dallas didn't know how Tony would figure it out, but somehow he would. Maybe he already knew. He sounded like he knew something. Tony was smart. And Tony was nobody to mess with. Fortunately, the plan Dallas had worked out would take care of Tony.

Dallas, for the first time in his life, would get the last laugh on Tony. Even if he had to include Locaster in the plan, getting back at Tony would be worth it.

But if Tony figured out about the strip club and told the bikers, Dallas was dead.

Tonight was important. Play tonight right, and all his problems would be over. Wanda would be in Holbrook. He pictured her in Tepee Number One.

Once Locaster was out of the picture, things would be different. Dallas could see Wanda looking around at what he'd done with The Sunset. She'd be impressed. Anyone would be impressed with Tepee Number One. Shag carpet and a big round bed. He'd gotten the inspiration from a picture in *Life Magazine* featuring Wilt Chamberlain's bachelor pad. It wasn't easy to get the round bed into the tepee, but once he got it in the door it fit real nice.

If it was good enough for Wilt the Stilt, it was good enough for the *Big D*.

COUNTY COURTHOUSE

"You know if Merlinda's working today?"

Deputy Lot Conover, working security at the front of the new county complex wasn't sure if Merlinda was there today, but he did know Merlinda. Just like he knew the big guy standing in front of him was none other than Dallas King.

Conover eyed Dallas. The motel magnate wore a guayaberra, fancy looking designer jeans, a pair of loafers with gold chains over the vamps. His blonde hair came down over his ears like you would see on a television variety show singer.

Lot Conover knew all the courthouse employees. He had a memory second to none. He remembered who had been arrested over the years by which deputy and what they had been charged with. In some ways, his memory was photographic. But he was also discrete. Conover didn't trumpet all his knowledge to the world like some other deputies. Some deputies told their wives everything, which guaranteed everyone in town heard everything happening at the sheriff's office.

Conover believed *nobody* needed to know *anything*. The principle worked well for him. He knew Dallas King by sight, but he would be damned if he would greet him by name. Instead, Conover gave Dallas a look like there was somebody directly behind him standing in the hall. Conover sure as hell wasn't telling this Howdy Doody anything.

Conover hated thinking Merlinda was mixed up with Dallas King. She was a good girl from a good family. Some connection to Joe Beach, Conover thought. Shame for her to get involved with Dallas King. She'd just gotten away from Dallas's cousin. Granted, Tony King was probably worse, but Dallas had the smell of something really bad on him. Dallas had the stink of a crime covered up. Conover looked warily at Dallas. Something about the guayaberra and the fancy blonde hair.

Who could say Dallas wasn't worse than Tony?

Conover knew all about Tony. He had taught Tony some manners once.

But Dallas was sneaky

Tony was a rattlesnake, but at least a rattler gives a warning.

Dallas might be something worse.

"Haven't seen her today," Conover said.

He leaned back in a wooden chair he had grabbed from the industrial arts classroom of the high school when they upgraded. Conover liked the chair. Its simple wooden design could take Conover's weight. It looked like an electric chair without the doo-dads. Behind Conover, photographs of the county sheriffs lined the wall.

Deputy Lot Conover was older than the current sheriff. With his big turquoise bola tie and the Model 10 holstered on his hip, Lot Conover fit in better with the pictures of the older sheriffs.

He squinted at Dallas.

"You gonna fix up that place you got?"

Dallas shuffled his feet. Looked surprised at the question.

"The Sunset? It's fine. Showers, sinks, and such. Come on over, I'll show you."

"The air conditioning in those back units don't work, I can make a call and get you shut down yesterday."

Dallas smiled.

"Just fixed everything, boss. Come on down, I'll take you on a tour."

Conover leaned forward. All four chair legs met the floor.

He scowled at Dallas.

"She works in the recorder's office. Down the hall, turn right. No smoking in there. Watch out for the head lady. She's out for blood today. You light up a smoke, she'll make you wish you never been born."

Dallas laughed.

"Thanks again, boss."

Conover stood up.

"One more thing, boyo. You mess with that girl, you'll wish you hadn't."

Conover stared at Dallas.

"You hear what I'm saying?"

Dallas held up both palms toward Conover.

"Honest, I got it. I just need to give her a message from a friend."

"Your cousin?"

"No way," Dallas said. "You know Edison Graves?"

Conover nodded.

If Dallas was telling the truth, that was fine.

Conover knew Edison Graves.

There was no harm in Edison.

BIGGER FISH

"She didn't come in today, and she didn't call."

The tall woman wore shoulder pads under her fuchsia blazer. She reminded Dallas of Aunt Fritzi in the Nancy cartoons. She wasn't overly happy about talking with Dallas. She looked over her glasses at him and shook her head.

"See, the thing is," Dallas said, "normally, I wouldn't bother her at work, but there's something that's come up that's really important that she finds out without me having to come back. I mean, I *can* come back, if she's going to be coming in, but, you know, it would maybe be better if I could talk to her right now, if you know what I mean, so if you could give me her phone number, or where she lives…"

Dallas gave his most engaging grin.

"I'm sorry, sir," the woman said. "It's absolutely impossible for me to say more to you, without Merlinda's permission."

"She's a friend of the family," Dallas said. "How's she gonna give you permission to talk if she's not here? I gotta give her a message, see? That's the whole thing."

"She should be here, today. She's on *probation*," the woman said.

Like that settled something.

"She's not a regular employee. She is here on *probation*. If you see her, you should tell her she's not doing herself any favors by being absent today."

The woman looked at Dallas and frowned.

"I have no idea where Merlinda lives. I wouldn't be able to tell you if I did. I wouldn't, if I could."

The woman hesitated.

"If you want, write a message. I'll put it on the desk where she's *supposed* to be working. When she comes in, she'll see it."

Dallas shook his head. He did not want to write anything.

"The thing is, she needs to get the message today for it to do any good. It's real important."

Dallas looked directly into the woman's gray eyes.

"I think she has to give blood, and she's the only person with the right blood type. Something like that, anyway."

The woman sighed.

"She isn't here. I don't know if she will be here. I could spell it out for you, but I'm not sure that would help, so if you will excuse me, I will wish you the best of luck."

"She has a rare blood type."

"Oh dear," the woman said. "That is unfortunate."

Dallas nodded. That just about covered it.

He walked back down the hallway, turned the corner to where Deputy Conover had resumed leaning his chair under the gallery of sheriffs.

"Find her?" Conover said.

Conover was smiling.

Maybe he heard the woman. Dallas couldn't tell.

Dallas pushed the door open and went back into the sunshine. He wanted to go back and say something to Conover.

Who the hell did Conover think he was, anyway?

The fresh air felt good after the stultifying atmosphere of the courthouse.

Dallas got behind the wheel of his Coupe de Ville. He pulled his mirrored sunglasses from the breast pocket of the guayaberra.

Conover should have been put out to pasture a long time ago, but like everything else in this town, it wasn't who you were, it was who you knew. Conover knew everyone. He obviously knew Dallas, but still gave him the once-over like he might have given a hobo who had drifted into town on a freight train.

Dallas didn't like that one little bit, but Conover's opinion of him was of no concern.

Who cared what the old has-been thought?

Dallas got the car and air conditioning going and rolled down his window.

He had bigger fish to fry than Conover.

He almost didn't see her.

The small woman stood next to the passenger side of the Coupe de Ville.

Dallas had noticed her when he came out of the recorder's office. She must have followed him out here.

She clutched two files in front of her blouse, shifting her feet in the dusty parking lot. Sweating a little, just like everybody else in this heat but maybe in her case a little more. Maybe from the exertion of catching up, more likely from nervousness.

She wore tight Wrangler jeans, and her hair swept up and back from her forehead.

"You need to get in touch with Merlinda?"

Dallas nodded.

"That's why I came here, anyway," he said. "It's important."

"I won't tell you where she is," the woman said. "She's trying to get away from Tony."

The woman kept the files in front of her as if protecting herself from Dallas.

Dallas smiled.

"I don't need to see her if you can get her a message."

"Depends," the woman said.

"You know Edison Graves?"

The woman smiled.

"Everybody knows Edison. Merlinda and him were something together. She should be with him instead of Tony."

Dallas nodded.

"Tony's crazy, you know?" The woman looked straight at Dallas. "He wants to know where she is. That's why she's not coming in. He could kill her."

Dallas smiled. He wanted to look sympathetic.

"I don't need to know where she is," he said. "But Edison really needs to see her. He'll be in town tonight. He'll be at the Ten High tonight at seven. Can you tell her that?"

"Edison *Graves*?" the woman said.

Dallas nodded.

"He's coming up for a rodeo," he said.

The woman smiled, but only slightly.

"I'll tell her," she said.

MAMA TRIED

The truck was hot.

Edison pulled the keys from the visor, rolled the window down, and started the F-150.

Dallas's phone call made him think about Merlinda.

He liked Merlinda, but it just hadn't worked into anything.

Indian Wells wasn't just another rodeo. Indian Wells was a nice rodeo. Good people. Maybe one of the first he'd gone to with Livingston.

He could hear the announcer and remember the excitement he felt being at the rodeo with his big brother.

He had been a kid. Not even thirteen.

Green, but Edison would have been willing to get up on any horse and take whatever punishment came his way.

Livingston taught him.

Edison told himself to quit his bitching and cowboy up.

Why did he have the foreboding feeling? The prickling sensation felt like somebody was walking on Edison's grave.

Maybe it was the way Jane told him to be careful.

Don't get yourself killed.

He couldn't afford to think like that.

Rodeo is a dangerous sport.

Like racing a stock car, which he had never done.

Or returning a punt, which he had.

Danger was part of rodeo.

If he started concentrating on what *could* happen, he would be a fool to ever take another ride.

Better to approach things with fatalism.

Ride the horse as long as you can.

Kiss the ladies no matter what.

Edison slotted an 8-track in the deck of his pickup. Wedged it in with a pack of matches he'd grabbed when he left Jane's. Merle Haggard's greatest album of all time. *Mama Tried,* from 1969. Another tape from Livingston's shoebox filled with classics. Edison had practically worn the tape out listening to the title song.

I turned twenty-one in prison.

Edison turned up the volume.

Life without parole.

Edison hadn't turned twenty-one in prison, thanks to Livingston.

❋ ❋ ❋

At the trailer, Edison pulled down the beige shades to keep the heat out, knowing he was pissing in the wind. Without air circulation, the Airstream would heat up to a temperature rivaling the wood fired kiln.

Edison checked the refrigerator finding nothing but a Dr Pepper and two cans of Schlitz.

He checked his gloves, rigging, chaps, and spurs and packed them carefully in his wooden footlocker then picked it up onto his shoulder and carried it outside.

He hesitated momentarily and then took his .38.

After locking his gear in the diamond plate utility box he'd bolted into the bed of the pickup Edison, hefted his saddle onto his shoulder and put it on the passenger's side. His cowboy hat was on the rack behind his seat.

It was his lucky hat. Edison wouldn't compete without it.

He took off the bandanna he'd been wearing and put on the Stetson. He hadn't forgotten a thing.

Edison Graves was ready for the three hour drive.

❊ ❊ ❊

Holbrook, Arizona isn't that far from Globe, but Edison hadn't been there for a while. His growing up years weren't perfect, but Edison had accomplished things he was proud of. Playing football had gotten him out of Holbrook. He'd earned a bachelor's degree at the U of A after leaving Dartmouth. He was working on his masters.

He made money down in the mines. He had learned to make silver jewelry and had finally finished making the flute he'd been working on when he met Trinity. Edison wouldn't have gotten as far as he had if he'd stayed in Holbrook.

There were other things. He had been a ring dancer, a bronc rider, he could give and take a punch. Edison Graves was one tough son-of-a-bitch.

He was proud of most but not all of what he'd done in his life.

Holbrook was as close as Edison had to a home.

He'd grown up there, but it hadn't been easy.

LONESOME BUCKAROOS

The Ten High Saloon was dead. Forrest Canyon looked above the bar and saw an A-1 beer sign, the one with the cowboy dreaming. The clouds above the cowboy's head formed a naked lady if you looked hard enough. The bar was shaped like an L with the bottom part being the stage and dance floor and the top part where tables were set up. A skinny little corridor to the side looked like there was a cigarette machine wedged in there and a pay phone before you got to the men's room. The women's was somewhere else and Forrest had no concern about that.

He walked in like he owned the place and set the Fender amp up on the stage before going over to the bartender, a salty looking character with a patch over his right eye. The guy was watching a television game show hosted by Gene Rayburn. Forrest would have liked to get on one of those shows. He felt like he could do well, with his steady nerves and all. He thought maybe he'd do that when he got to California. He wasn't sure how far Bakersfield was from Burbank, but figured it would be worth the drive if he could make some money.

He wouldn't go on Let's Make a Deal, though. Standing around like a jackass in a scarecrow costume was beneath his dignity. No Monty Hall or Carol Merrill for Forrest.

He just plain wouldn't do it.

❖ ❖ ❖

"You with the band? Didn't know they had a steel guitar."

The bartender was talking to Forrest.

Forrest looked up. After a minute he'd found the outlets by the stage.

Forrest had the plugs in and the Sho Bud out. Played a quick, recognizable lick. The opening bars of Tammy Wynette's *D-I-V-O-R-C-E*. Everybody knew that lick. It was like Beethoven or something. Everybody recognized it.

"Just doing a sound check," Forrest said.

Which basically didn't mean shit.

The bartender went back to doing nothing but watching the television.

Forrest played some more. Damn, he sounded good tonight. The acoustics in the bar made him sound great.

"What are you doing, partner?"

A big man with a red beard and a potbelly stood in front of Forrest, holding a Fender case and a can of Schlitz.

"Just passing through, man. Heard y'all was short a steel."

The big man laughed. "We ain't got nothing like that. Just yours truly and a couple others."

Forrest played the intro bars to "*Lonesome Fugitive*." Merle's lead was on a Telecaster, but the Sho-Bud made it sound ten times better.

"Guess I heard wrong then. Sorry 'bout that."

Forrest stood up.

The big man held up his palm.

"Hold on, now. You want to sit in tonight, that would be fine. Can't pay you. Maybe give you a split of the tips tonight plus a little."

Forrest grinned. Sat back down.

"That would be just fine, mister."

The men shook hands.

Forrest put his hands back on his steel guitar.

The big man glanced down.

The words *GOOD LUCK* were tattooed above Forrest's knuckles.

THE MODEL 10

Lot Conover's horse was used to the afternoon ritual.

Molly was the gentle mare Conover had ridden for the more than ten years since the death of his wife, Darlene.

Conover remembered sitting next to the radio with his grandfather, listening to Bill Monroe sing *Molly and Tenbrooks*.

Conover's grandfather built his house out of good adobe. He constructed the fireplace out of the petrified wood found on his ranch. His grandfather was a lawman and Conover followed in his footsteps.

Conover couldn't remember a time when he'd thought of doing anything else. He came to the conclusion late in life everything had happened to him in precisely the right order. He would not be riding this horse through the upcoming gate if he had done anything differently.

Conover was a man who believed he was still walking this earth for a special reason.

The belief helped when bouts of despondency threatened to overtake him.

He knew he had one more errand to run before he died.

Thoughts like this came frequently to Conover. He wasn't sure if it was age or because his wife had died early.

They said his wife went to glory.

He remembered the words from her funeral, and how he'd coughed, hearing them.

She'd been in her glory here on the ranch, and Conover missed her like anything.

❈ ❈ ❈

He barely needed to touch the reins.

Molly knew every step of the ride behind the corral. She knew where they were headed.

Conover and Molly rode through the gate between Conover's ranch and the grazing land.

❈ ❈ ❈

Conover didn't consider himself old. He could pull his weight in any detail, but since Darlene had died, he'd fought hard against depression. The new sheriff wasn't making things easy for Conover, either.

Sheriff Jenkins thought he was doing Conover a favor by reducing his duty. Conover was used to a lot more action.

Of course, Conover could always be called out to

respond to incidents close by, but those happened rarely and were usually handled by the police department.

※ ※ ※

Conover looked across the painted desert sky.

Molly stepped gingerly over the bars of the cattle crossing. Below the grate, debris had gathered in the ditch. Lotaburger wrappers. Nothing stopped the wind. They could have come from Gallup, almost a hundred miles away.

Molly was gentle and sensitive. She trusted Conover.

Conover slid out of the saddle and stroked the horse.

From his saddle bag, Conover pulled out a six and a half ounce bottle of Coca Cola.

Forty paces away, Conover kept two bales of straw.

He didn't need to see the paper targets on the bales. He knew their relative positions.

Conover walked away from Molly.

Molly was used to the sound of gunfire.

He used a Smith and Wesson Model 10. One of thousands made. Conover saw no reason to change to the 686. The Model 10 was a practical handgun, perfect for it's function. In Conover's hands it was as accurate as it needed to be.

He loaded the Model 10.

Six cartridges fit in the revolver's cylinder. Back

in the days of single actions, lawmen often carried only five to prevent mishaps in the brush, but Conover's grandfather always loaded six.

"Be a shame to ever come up short, Lot," his grandfather said.

Sometimes Conover could still hear his grandfather's voice.

Speed wasn't Conover's primary concern. Fancy tricks were for Wild West shows, not for Lot Conover.

Doing things right was his primary concern. He turned and stared at the targets. Their image impressed itself into his consciousness. Lot Conover turned away from the target.

The gun cleared leather and the bullets tore into the targets. Three shots in one, three in the second.

There was no finer gunhand than Conover.

The shots hardly startled the horse. She and Conover came out every night.

He pulled the stirrup up and used the side to open the Coke. Conover sipped the warm soda. Pulled a half carrot from his pocket and gave it to his horse. He put the bottle back in the saddle bags. He would clean the gun at home.

Every night was the same. Conover would ride the horse into the desert, fire the pistol, clean it when he returned.

He grabbed the saddle horn and lifted himself up onto the horse. He felt the horse's movement as she adjusted to Conover's weight. Conover settled himself into the saddle.

He was getting hungry. The first streaks of orange and purple appeared in the sky.

Conover was getting older. The stiffness in his joints and pains from old injuries were coming back like old, uninvited guests.

There might not be any reason to continue his gun practice. He would never have a problem with the annual departmental qualification.

Sheriff Jenkins said Conover was done with active investigations.

He could continue in the courthouse until retirement came. Desk work.

But Conover was a gunman with a history and he knew history could return, just like the old injuries, and like the pain he felt when Darlene died.

There were people who held grudges against Conover.

He wouldn't end his life as a victim of a half-witted criminal with a gun.

Lot Conover would defend himself.

Conover patted Molly.

"Come on girl," he said. "Time to head home."

GREEN, GREEN GRASS OF HOME

Leaving Globe, Edison would have said the temptation of the rodeo arena got him out on Route 60 and made him wind his way through the Salt River Canyon before reaching the ponderosa pines of the White Mountains.

Even before hitting the city limits of Holbrook, Edison knew he wasn't riding for money.

Edison wanted the chance to prove something.

The rodeo was a connection with his dead brother. Hearing the announcer call his name, seeing the crowd in the stands. It all took Edison back to his early days with Livingston.

The purse was chicken scratch, barely worth getting into his truck.

The Merle Haggard tape was in the deck.

Green, Green Grass of Home.

Edison drove the pickup down Hopi Boulevard. The town's main street not as busy this time of night as in the old days.

Neon lights bathed the street in circus colors

designed to lure tired tourists in with promises of ice cold air conditioning and refreshing swimming pools.

A maroon Mercury cut in front of Edison. Edison swerved, slamming his brakes to avoid hitting the car.

"Son-of-a-bitch," Edison said.

A blonde woman in the passenger seat rolled down her window. She was about to say something to Edison. On the other side of the Mercury the driver turned toward Edison. Dark hair and mustache. A long thin face.

A Tiparillo cigar hanging from the man's lips.

Edison took a deep breath. The woman said something to the driver and the Mercury did a quick turn into Dallas's motel.

The Sunset Motel.

The orange neon sign above the office flashed.

Vacancy.

THE STAGECOACH STEAK HOUSE

Adrenalin rushed to Edison's brain.

Rage filled his body.

He looked at the Mercury again. Trying to cool himself down.

The couple were staying at Dallas's motel.

Dallas would come out to see the woman.

Edison pulled off the road across from the motel into the parking lot of the Stagecoach Steak House.

Edison turned the ignition key off. From his truck, he looked across the boulevard at the Sunset Motel.

The driver stood outside the car. He wore a beige leisure suit and a pair of gold aviator glasses. Thinning hair cut long over the ears. A sandy mustache.

He was walking deliberately into the office of the Sunset Motel, one foot stepping in front of the other like a cat.

The man held a lighted Tiparillo and was knocking on the door of the Sunset's office.

The woman stood on the concrete in front of the office.

Blonde, wearing a T-shirt and ripped jeans.

Much younger than the man.

The woman crossed her arms and looked down the street as if expecting a ride to arrive.

The traffic was steady. Mostly westbound. One car slowed down next to the motel.

The driver appraised the woman who then turned away.

The car drove off.

If Dallas saw her he would come out, rolling up his sleeves, ready to help.

The Good Samaritan.

The neon light gave the woman an eerie appearance. She took a cigarette from a leather pouch.

Smoke curled toward the motel's neon sign.

The man was in the motel office with Dallas.

Edison couldn't see what they were doing. The angle wasn't right. All Edison could see was the brightly lit office counter.

Dallas and the man were standing away from the window.

Edison thought about moving the truck for a better view then decided not to.

This was none of his business.

The man was in the office for a while.

Another car slowed down then continued back

into traffic quickly.

The woman walked back to the Mercury and took a small bag from the back seat. Maybe a makeup case. It was about the right size and shape.

She balanced it on the trunk.

There were rooms available. Most of the motel was unoccupied. The man had still not come back out from the office. Edison wondered how long the woman would wait out on the street.

How long would she wait before getting into one of the cars heading west?

Dallas and the man moved into sight. The man stood talking to Dallas. He and Dallas were talking and moving their hands like they knew each other. The man pointed toward the car. Dallas said something and the man called to the woman.

She turned her back, continuing to rummage through the cosmetic case.

The man came back outside and said something to the woman. They both went to the back of the car. The man opened the trunk and took out two suitcases. They started to walk toward the rooms.

Edison looked at the Stagecoach Steak House. He was hungry. A steak sounded good and he was in no hurry to see Dallas.

Edison got out of the truck. Putting the keys under the visor, he pulled up his jeans and went into the steak house.

The waitress smiled. She wore a black skirt and a white blouse. The Friday night crowd would be in later. Muzak played overhead.

Seasons in the Sun.

In the entry, black and white photographs showed Holbrook during territorial days. The town hadn't changed much.

Edison didn't recognize the waitress.

"Sit anywhere you like," she said.

Edison took a seat in front of the plate glass window. The waitress put a menu and wine list in front of him.

He slid the wine list in the direction of the stagecoach salt and pepper shakers, focusing on the menu while looking out the window.

The couple in the Mercury were back under the motel sign. The man was still smoking a Tiparillo.

He looked angry. He was talking to the blonde, maybe explaining something to her.

She turned away from him, throwing her head back.

Dallas came out of the motel office.

The Stagecoach offered T-bone, London broil, or filet mignon. All with salad bar and potato included.

Dallas chatted with the couple.

Using his hands.

Dallas could sell somebody their own car.

Edison looked at the salad bar's eight silver bins set in ice. Looked at the clear plastic sneeze bar across the top. The steak house was empty.

Edison was the first customer of the night.

Dallas had to be selling something.

Always selling.

Dallas and his Tilt-a-Whirl.

Edison looked back at the menu.

He would see Dallas soon enough.

Edison wondered if the angle of the sun in the early evening had brought out the melancholy streak he was feeling.

He was starting to think about the rodeo and why he had come to Holbrook.

The waitress came to his table, holding a basket of bread sticks and ranch dressing.

Edison remembered his first rodeo. He'd drawn a crazy paint and been thrown almost immediately.

But the excitement carried him into the next round, and the next round after that.

A rush of energy.

Edison started to feel it again.

Edison nodded toward the window.

"You know that guy?"

The waitress nodded.

"Dallas? Are you kidding? Everybody knows Dallas."

Edison laughed.

"Yeah, that's him all right. What's your name?"

The waitress put the basket down.

"Piper," she said. "You know Dallas?"

"Piper," Edison said. "Yeah, I know Dallas. Everybody knows Dallas."

She laughed.

"Big D, he's calling himself."

Edison laughed.

"Big D, huh?"

Piper nodded. A quick smile.

"You look familiar," she said. "Do you live here?"

"While back. My name's Edison Graves."

"Okay, Edison," Piper said.

Dallas and the couple were talking. Dallas went back into the office and brought out a key.

Dallas was looking at the woman.

Talking to the man while looking at the woman.

Edison handed the menu back to Piper.

"T-bone. Medium rare. Baked potato."

She nodded. All business now.

"Comes with the salad bar. You can get started with that whenever you want."

Edison nodded toward the window.

Piper looked at the three people under the neon sign.

Edison raised his eyebrows.

"What do *you* think, Piper? He's some kind of out-of-town business man? Brings his wife here occasionally?"

She looked back through the window.

Laughed.

"You're kidding, right?"

Edison grinned.

Piper turned toward the kitchen.

"I forgot to light the candle on your table."

"I can do it," Edison said. He dug in his pocket for his Zippo.

"He may be a businessman," she said. "But she's

not his wife."

Edison looked out the window. The man was carrying a long guitar case toward the rooms. The woman walked next to him, bumping his hip slightly.

Dallas still stood under the light of the motel's neon sign, watching the couple until they reached their room.

"I'll put in the order for your steak," Piper said. "Shouldn't take long. You want more bread sticks, I can get 'em for you."

The man and the woman stood in front of the door of their room. They were arguing. He held her arm, then she pulled it away and started to walk toward their car.

The man said something.

It was like watching a silent movie.

The woman turned back, heading toward the man who now had the door open.

She wasn't happy.

The woman was coming back under protest.

Piper was right.

This was no wife.

THE TEN HIGH SALOON

Leaving the keys to the red and white pickup in the visor, Edison pulled up his jeans and stood outside the Ten High. The Ten High Saloon's swinging doors and brass rails had been a landmark since territorial days.

A few years ago, the Ten High Saloon had been packed nearly every night of the week.

When travelers took Route 66 from Illinois to California, cars regularly pulled into the parking lot just outside Holbrook.

Parched travelers got out to stretch and get some gas, stand in the sun, decide if they wanted to keep going.

The Ten High was a place to drink cold beer and listen to honky tonk music.

The Bucket of Blood had been more famous, but it had long since closed it's doors.

Station wagons, sedans, trucks, and motorcycles still filled the parking lot of the Ten High on weekends.

Hollywood never put Holbrook on the map. The town was never as notorious as Tombstone, but plenty of blood had been shed in the frontier town. A lot of it had been spilled in the Ten High.

The adobe walls outside the saloon had been painted with a map of Route 66. Some of the towns mentioned in that song were painted in red.

Gallup New Mexixo.
Flagstaff, Arizona.
Don't forget Winona.

Then in bigger letters:

Last Beer 'Til Winslow.

The Ten High had been a major watering hole on Route 66 back in the good old days. Since the arrival of I-40 Holbrook had lost business. Perched between Gallup and Winslow, Holbrook had once been a natural stop. Gas, cold drinks and motel rooms were available, and a quick trip to the Painted Desert and the Petrified Forest.

Holbrook still had ranching and the railroad, and being the county seat, the courthouse and jail were there.

Edison felt the sweat and dust he'd picked up from the ride north. The high desert evening would cool down soon.

He pulled his bandanna from his back pocket, circled his face, and felt for his wallet. He had plenty of cash, but didn't plan on a long evening.

Edison wasn't a big drinker. He would drink a beer or two, but he didn't like getting drunk.

He wouldn't be staying late tonight. He would need sleep before the rodeo.

Standing in the crowded parking lot, Edison heard music from the bar. Weekends meant live music. Edison pushed his hat up and walked into the bar.

Dim Lights, Thick Smoke.

Loud, loud, loud.

The band was rocking.

Two women were on the floor dancing. It was early. The band was a drummer, a bass player, and an old white guy with a red beard named Bobby Stover.

Bobby Stover played a cream colored Telecaster strapped over his big belly. Bobby had played in Holbrook forever.

Bobby had a pedal steel guy sitting in.

Edison didn't recognize *him*. He wore a polyester shirt buttoned to the top, dark glasses, and a greased pompadour. He could flat-out *play* steel guitar.

His Sho-Bud steel guitar, inlaid with mother-of-pearl, glistened through the dim lights and thick smoke of the bar. Across his knuckles the words *GOOD LUCK* were tattooed in Olde English script.

Like a lot of the pedal steel players Edison had seen, the guy looked a little shady. Edison watched him play. He looked familiar, like Edison had seen him on television.

Edison scuffed his boot on the floor, checking to see if the surface was okay for dancing.

Merlinda liked to dance.

If she came here.

If she didn't, Edison would still dance.

Why not?

Eat, drink, and be merry.

Tomorrow, he could die.

Nobody to dance with yet. Maybe the girls from the bank would come in like he remembered.

Just like they did everywhere.

Maybe girls from Winslow or even Gallup.

Dallas might have lied about Merlinda.

She probably wouldn't come here.

Edison found a booth and sat down.

Dallas King came up to the booth.

Edison hadn't seen him.

Dallas had put on some weight. He was still parting his blonde hair like Glen Campbell.

He slid a longneck beer in front of Edison.

"Glad you came up, Edison. Glad I went ahead and called you."

Edison shook Dallas's hand.

Dallas broke away and clicked his fingers. Fishing out a smoke, he lighted it, then pulled a business card from the cellophane of the pack and flicked it toward Edison.

"Got some new cards made up. Take a look."

Edison looked at the card.

Dallas "Big D" King.

Dallas was calling himself a consultant.

A consultant? Edison thought. Dallas was a slumlord carny.

Dallas had gotten himself a new tattoo on his forearm.

Big D.

Olde English lettering like the pedal steel player.

"No reason to stay away, Edison," Dallas said. "You should come up more."

Edison laughed.

"I'm just here for the rodeo, Dallas. Tell me what you're gonna tell me cause I can't stay too long. Gotta get back to Globe by Monday. Doesn't look like anything has changed around here."

"Nothing changes here," Dallas said. "Not much, anyway."

Edison took a swig from the bottle.

"Why don't you just go ahead and tell me what you need to tell me. I may not stick around here tonight."

"Serious," Dallas said. "You're still going to Indian Wells tomorrow then?"

"I'll pay you back for the entry fee," Edison said. "Got my gear in the truck. Why not?"

"It's a good little rodeo," Dallas said. "Don't worry about the entry. It's on me. You just ride."

✻ ✻ ✻

Edison probably wouldn't have noticed the

couple if he hadn't seen them earlier in front of Dallas's motel.

They were sitting across the dance floor now.

Edison looked at the couple.

Then Dallas pointed them out.

Not subtly, either.

The man still had the hangdog look and the Tiparillo. Mod haircut and aviator glasses. He could have been a fixture in any lounge across the country.

Dallas pointed at the woman.

"How about them apples?" Dallas said. "She's about as nice as they get, don't you think, Edison?"

Edison glanced at the couple then turned back to Dallas.

"No man," Dallas said. "Take a *real* look, Edison. Take a look at her. Nice, huh?"

The man got up and said something to the blonde. She looked bored.

Edison nodded. It might be time to leave.

Dallas was getting worked up. His face was flushed.

"Look at her, wouldja? That's what *I'm* talking about."

The man looked over. Stepped toward the pool table then changed his mind. He turned back to the table and tugged at the blonde's arm.

There was a wobble in the man's stride. Maybe drunk.

Edison shrugged.

"I guess so, Dallas. If you say so."

"Damn right she's nice. She's as nice as they get. She's interested, too, brother."

The woman stood up and the man put his arm around her waist.

If the man wasn't drunk, he was close.

Dallas gave Edison a look.

"They're staying at my place. I had my eye on her since they first came in. Put them in Number Two. Right where I can keep my eye on her."

"Looks like she's with him, Dallas. Looks like you're out of luck."

The band was playing a song Edison didn't recognize featuring the steel guitar player.

"Watch me, bro," Dallas said. "See what kind of luck I got."

The blonde woman and the tall man were dancing.

Dallas was right. The woman looked okay.

Not stop the world, but nice.

Dallas kept looking at her.

❋ ❋ ❋

Edison was about to give up on seeing Merlinda. He was about to leave when she came to his booth.

How long since he'd seen Merlinda? Five years? Six?

"Hey Edison," she said.

Edison looked up and after a second, slid over to make room for her.

Just as if she'd seen him every day for the last

few years.

"Merlinda," he said.

He felt a little bashful and he didn't know why.

Edison tried to act naturally.

Sliding the long neck between the palms of his hands like he came into the Ten High all the time.

Like he'd seen Merlinda a few days ago instead of a few years.

❊ ❊ ❊

"It's been a long time, hasn't it?" Merlinda said.

"A hell of a long time, Merlinda," Edison said. "What you been up to then?"

"You know," she said. "This and that."

Edison shook his head.

Whatever she'd been doing, it looked good on her.

She looked at him.

"How about you, Edison?"

"Same old thing, Merlinda," he said. "Played football back east then came home. I been working in Globe at the mine. Rodeoing when I get a chance."

He skipped the part about Livingston.

Either she knew about Livingston or she didn't.

"Still?" Merlinda said.

She gave him a look.

"Still," he said. "Riding tomorrow."

He pulled out a cigarette.

"Globe's not far. You ever been down there?"

"Course I been to Globe, Edison. I've been every last place in this state."

Edison laughed.

"You always come back here, though."

"My grandfather," she said.

"I'd like to see him," Edison said.

He lighted the cigarette.

"He's up there, Edison," she said. "You know where he lives."

"You here by yourself, Merlinda?"

Merlinda laughed.

"You're asking if I have a boyfriend?"

He was beginning to feel more comfortable.

"Yeah," he said. "I guess I am."

"I had a boyfriend, but we broke up. Then I heard you were going to be here."

Edison nodded.

"You still riding horses?"

"Course I am," she said.

"Barrel racing?"

She nodded.

"I got my horse over at the fairground at the stables," Merlinda said. "That guy Calvin is taking care of her."

Edison remembered watching her ride. Merlinda knew what she was doing.

"Same pretty little horse?"

"Same one. She's doing fine."

"That's good," he said "She's a good one."

Edison patted Merlinda's hand.

She smiled.

Shyly, as if they had just been introduced.

The waitress brought another Schlitz.

Edison pointed at the beer.

"Want one of these?"

She shook her head.

"Maybe in a little while."

"You want to dance, Merlinda?"

"Not yet. I just want to talk for a minute, Edison. I can't stay."

She settled against the back of the booth, her white blouse contrasting with the dark red vinyl.

"That's fine, Merlinda," Edison said. "Just wait till they play some dancing music and I'll get you up there."

"Edison," she said, "I'm glad to see you."

They sat at the booth. They were alone and Edison liked that.

The band started Ernest Tubb's *Walking the Floor Over You*.

Edison stood up. "Come on, Merlinda. Ernest Tubb. We gotta dance now."

They made a nice couple, two-stepping in the dim light of the Holbrook bar.

Sawdust on the floor, a neon Miller sign behind them.

They danced until the song came to an end and then stood while some other couples left the floor.

Merlinda and Edison waited.

As if they knew, the band started to play a slow one. A Commodores song.

Merlinda felt good in Edison's arms.

Three Times a Lady.

They swayed gently to the sentimental song. Edison put his hat on Merlinda's head. Over her shoulder, Edison saw the tall man and the blonde dancing. Edison looked at them. The man was slow dancing with the blonde, but he glared at Edison.

He looked angry as hell.

Edison kept dancing.

Nothing to worry about.

With Merlinda in his arms everything felt all right.

PAY PHONE

Dallas looked at Edison and Merlinda.

A nice reunion.

The two of them were getting along really nice. Things were going well.

The hall between the dance floor and the men's room was narrow and smoky.

Dallas dug in his pocket and grabbed a quarter. He slid it into the pay phone. The place needed a coat of paint. Numbers written on this wall probably went all the way back to Route 66 days.

He pulled a bandanna from his back pocket and placed it over the phone. Punched in the numbers. Heard the coins drop. He checked his watch.

Quarter after seven.

The plan was in motion. No going back.

Tony answered after two rings.

"Yeah?"

Dallas spoke with an exaggerated imitation of a native voice.

"Merlinda's your old lady?"

"Yeah," Tony said. "Who's this?"

"If Merlinda's your old lady you should see her tonight, then."

Nothing.

Tony didn't say a thing.

Dallas held the phone out so Tony could hear some of the sounds from the bar. He looked back at the booth where Edison and Merlinda were sitting.

"Merlinda looks like she's having a good time then," Dallas said. "You should see her. She's having such a good time with this guy, they're falling all over each other."

"Where you calling from, hoss?"

Dallas laughed. He looked back at Merlinda and Edison.

"She's at the Ten High. Least she is for now. Looks like she's about to go home with this cowboy. Maybe pretty soon, too."

"Who is this?"

The plan was working.

Dallas took the bandanna from the receiver. He wiped his hands and hung up the phone.

THE NEXT TEARDROP

Merlinda's finger's twined with Edison's. He was enjoying her company. The lights in the bar were dim and the cigarette smoke was thick. Edison looked at Merlinda. She looked even better than he remembered. Nostalgia could play tricks, but not this time.

He spoke louder to be heard over the music.

"You live around here, Merlinda?"

She nodded.

"Just staying here for now. Not too far. You look for it and you can find it."

Edison wasn't sure at all what that meant. He stood up. He should have just asked her where she was staying.

"I'll be back quick. Maybe we can walk somewhere."

She was looking at the band. Swaying a little with the music. The pedal steel was playing the chorus of that Freddie Fender song. The part right before Freddie starts singing in Spanish.

Before the Next Teardrop Falls.

"I'll be right back," Edison said.

※ ※ ※

The Ten High was as crowded as it ever got. The red vinyl booths were filled up as were the tables near the dance floor. The long mirror in back of the bar reflected the cowboys and Indians, the truck drivers and local yokels perched on the stools drinking draft beer. The mens room was crowded and it took a while for a urinal to free up.

Edison heard the sound of the steel guitar. It added a lot to the music. It transformed the house band from a little juke joint combo into something wild.

People were dancing out there.

Edison would give Merlinda a ride home if she wanted him to.

Did he really want to start anything up with Merlinda?

Edison didn't trust luck. Sometimes good fortune was just trouble's way of announcing itself.

Thinking too far into the future would push his luck. Better to just enjoy the night and stay out of trouble's way. Smile at Merlinda sitting with him.

He pulled out the knob for a pack of Newports outside the restroom, looking at Merlinda from a distance.

She looked better than ever.

Sitting not far from the edge of the dance floor.

She was wearing his cowboy hat and waiting for him.

He could think about the future later.

Right now, he was just glad she was here with him. He took another look at her.

"Why you looking at my old lady, Chief?"

Edison turned to face the tall man with the mustache. The same man he had watched at the Sunset Motel. The man in the Mercury with the blonde.

The man pushed Edison.

Edison fell back slightly then stepped toward the man.

"What are you talking about?" Edison said.

"Talking about this," the man said.

He twisted his right hand into a fist. Showed it to Edison. Edison laughed. The man *was* drunk. Edison grabbed the man's wrist and turned his arm with a quick motion. Edison held the twisted limb and felt the tendons in the man's arm stretch to the breaking point.

Even through an alcoholic haze, the man had to know his arm would snap unless Edison released him.

"Hey," the man said. "What the hell are you doing?"

Edison got up next to the man's face.

He applied a little more pressure to the arm then twisted.

The man's scream could barely be heard over

the music.

"I could kill you right now," Edison said. "Maybe I should."

Edison turned the man toward the machine and slammed his right knee into the man's kidney. A hard, precise shot. He held the man up and looked into his eyes.

"You gonna behave, or I gotta break this arm?"

"No, no," the man said.

"That's good," Edison said.

He let the man go.

Edison expected the man to go back to his table.

Instead, the man turned to Edison one more time.

Stuck his finger out.

"You think you can get away with this shit?"

Edison stepped to the side of the man. Cupped his hand. Chopped the man on his ear. The man would hear an echo for a while.

The man staggered and fell.

The band was playing *She Thinks I Still Care*.

Edison pulled the man up by the back of his belt. Walked him to the booth.

The blonde was smoking a cigarette. Watching the band. She didn't look concerned.

"I think he fell down or something," Edison said. "You better get him home."

The blonde woman looked at Edison. Opened her mouth as if to speak.

Said nothing.

* * *

Edison heard a commotion on the other end of the floor.

The band had been playing *Cotton Eyed Joe.*

He had gone to the bar to get Merlinda a drink.

New people were sitting where the couple had been.

Everything had gone back to normal.

Edison figured line dancing would be a good time to get Merlinda out of the place.

He didn't want to line dance. Merlinda might be willing to look at the stars.

He waited to get the bartender's attention. There were people in front of him.

The music was interrupted by crashes. The band stopped. People were shouting.

Edison couldn't make out what was being said. He walked away from the bar. The booth was empty

Empty long necks. Dead cigarette butts in the ashtray.

Merlinda was gone.

The band had stopped.

Dallas stood in front of Edison. He held two shot glasses.

He pushed one in front of Edison.

"Take this one, buddy. You missed all the shit. Tony just came in here like he was going to kill somebody."

Edison grabbed Dallas by the shirt.

"Where's Merlinda?" he said. "What happened."

He took the whiskey Dallas handed him and threw it back like it was nothing.

"Tony King," Dallas said.

"What about him?" Edison said.

"He just snatched Merlinda up like she was a rag doll. She didn't tell you about him?"

Edison shook his head no.

Dallas looked sad.

"She's been trying to get away from him, Edison," Dallas said. "I thought she'd done it, too."

PAWN SHOP

James Locaster knew what he was doing.

He reminded himself of a cat. All he'd needed was a glance of Tony.

Surfer boy's cousin. The one with the pawn shop.

His ear and his kidney hurt where the Indian hit him.

At Dallas's signal, Locaster had followed Tony and the girl.

Tony didn't look anything like Dallas. Tony was dark and there wasn't any fat on him.

By the time Wanda got up from the booth, Locaster had hit the door. He looked across the parking lot to where Tony stood holding the girl.

The big Indian had pissed him off with the sucker punch, but it was part of the plan. Dallas was going to dope the guy.

Anybody could see the Indian was violent.

Dallas came up with the idea of slipping the guy a mickey. He should have done it earlier in the evening. Locaster rubbed his back by his left kidney.

It hurt like hell where the guy kneed him.

Locaster got behind the wheel of the Ugly Duckling Mercury.

Wanda had already climbed into the back seat. She pushed her feet through the open window.

Giggling.

"Took you long enough."

"Sit up and watch this," Locaster said. "This should be good."

Locaster dug into the pocket of his pants and pulled out the car key. Twisted the key in the ignition and started the car.

Tony and the girl were standing in front of him. The one who'd been with the Indian.

Locaster knew what was coming.

Tony slapped the girl and Locaster saw her recoil. She tried pulling away from Tony.

Tony had her in a death grip.

"Watch this," Locaster said. "She's gonna get away."

The girl had some leverage.

She pulled her arm away from Tony.

Tony tried for another slap and missed.

Locaster heard Tony swear.

The girl ran down the alley.

Tony got into his truck.

IDENTICAL BARTENDERS

Edison ran out into the parking lot and watched Tony King's pickup leave the parking lot. Cutting through the dimly lit night, the truck left only dust and smoky exhaust behind.

He walked back into the bar. He picked up his hat from the floor.

His lucky hat. A pearl gray Stetson with a horsehair braid.

Merlinda had worn it.

He'd have to find out what happened.

Find out where Merlinda lived. Face down Tony.

Edison looked at the people milling around the bar.

He would have to look for Merlinda. He might get locked up or he might get killed, but he had to do it.

The bartender looked at Edison.

Edison felt woozy.

He stood with one of his boots propped on the brass rail.

He wasn't sure how he'd gotten there.

He remembered something about Merlinda, but wasn't sure what it was.

Two identical bartenders stood in front of Edison making identical motions.

A third bartender appeared.

All three bartenders stared at Edison.

Edison stabbed his thumb toward the booths.

He felt like he was spinning.

"You see what went on over there?" he said.

"That little lady got repoed," the bartender said. "Tony King's a tough hombre."

Edison nodded.

He closed his eyes briefly. He felt dizzy.

"You want something?" The bartender said.

The three bartenders looked at Edison.

Edison looked back to the booth where the man had been seated with the blonde.

They were gone.

Tony King, he thought.

Did he know Tony?

"Don't get too comfortable, buddy," the bartender said. "We're shutting down soon."

There was only one bartender now. The other two had faded away.

Edison closed one eye and focused on him.

"Kinda early, isn't it?"

The bartender shook his head.

"It's the law."

Edison closed both his eyes. Nothing looked right.

The bartender had changed. Edison didn't recognize him.

Edison backed away from the bar.
Hitched up his pants.
He needed to get to his truck.
He wouldn't be able to drive. He needed sleep.
His legs had turned to rubber.

HEADING TOWARD ROUTE 66

Other than neon lights from the motels, the town was dead.

Edison stood in front of the bar.

The pedal steel player came out the door and got into a Pontiac.

Dallas walked out and stood next to Edison.

"You all right, Edison? You gonna be ready to get going early tomorrow?"

Edison felt dizzy. He grabbed a post outside the bar and held it. His head was spinning. He was going to puke.

Edison closed his eyes.

Opened them.

Tried to focus on Dallas.

He held his fist up to Dallas then turned it into a two finger peace salute.

"You know where Merlinda lives then?"

Dallas shrugged.

"How would I know, Edison?"

Edison adjusted his hat and staggered away from Dallas.

Heading toward Route 66.

Edison needed to get to the desert.

The desert was his home.

Suddenly, everything seemed clear to Edison.

He would sleep in the desert tonight.

He had his bedroll and his wool blanket.

He would sleep under the star's canopy.

The constellations were up there to guide his steps.

Why hadn't he realized this before?

If he got cold, he would get back in his truck.

It was cold now.

He looked around.

Shook his head.

Things weren't as clear to Edison as they had been just moments before.

He should have looked for Merlinda.

He hadn't known about Tony King.

He hadn't known anything.

He still didn't.

❈ ❈ ❈

Edison stepped into the alley.

Where was he?

Everything was dark. Nothing looked right.

He needed to get to the desert.

Build a fire under the stars.

* * *

His truck wasn't where he'd parked it.
Edison kept going. He staggered across the alley then turned around.
Somebody was following him.
Merlinda?
He kept walking.
He hadn't parked the truck this far.
He walked farther, feeling his fists harden.
He was angry.
Angry enough to kill.

* * *

Edison felt the blow to his head.
Swirling red clouds spread before his eyes.
Black asphalt rose to meet him.
No stars shined in the purple sky.

CHLORAL HYDRATE

The mickey had made Edison wander into the alley and the blow to the back of his head brought him down to where he now lay next to the tailgate of his truck.

Dallas looked at him. Edison was unconscious. He wouldn't move for a while. The chloral hydrate had worked.

Dallas opened the tailgate of the truck. This was the tricky part. He looked at Edison. He was breathing. Dallas grabbed beneath Edison's shoulders. Pulled him up and propped his back against the tailgate. Dallas looked around. Nobody was near them.

If anyone came along Dallas was just moving his drunk buddy.

Just getting him home. He tried swinging Edison's boots and legs up onto the truck.

Nothing doing.

He needed to muscle Edison up into the bed of the truck. Dallas got his arms under Edison and lifted. He pushed him into the back and slid him forward. Slammed the tailgate.

Dallas found the truck keys under the visor.

Just like Livingston with the keys.

Dallas turned the key and the truck started.

Anybody stops me, I'm just driving old Edison back to my place to sleep it off.

He looked in the rear view mirror at the dark heap in the truck bed.

Edison wasn't moving.

OTHER VOICES

Edison felt something rolling underneath him. His whole body was moving. He was somewhere between consciousness and concussion. He had been hit with something heavy. Knocked out.

In the movies, Edison would have been out for hours.

This wasn't the movies.

He was being moved.

Edison couldn't tell where he was, but the stars above him were moving. He heard a sliding sound, then realized he was the one being slid.

He was in a covered wagon crossing the prairie.

He closed his eyes. Opened them when the movement stopped.

Closed his eyes again.

This time he kept them closed for a little longer.

He couldn't move.

He felt his body being picked up then dropped.

Somebody said something.

He heard other voices before drifting into darkness.

RED AND WHITE FORD F-150

Merlinda had gotten away from him.

Tony had slapped Merlinda and held her by the wrist, but she was stronger than he thought.

He underestimated her strength and she ripped away from him.

Cursed him.

She had never done that before.

She ran.

He started to follow, but stopped. There was no way Tony was going to outrun Merlinda.

Merlinda could run all day and all night if she wanted.

Tony would let her.

There were too many people around, anyway.

Cars were driving out of the parking lot. Drunks honking their way to the front.

Tony got back into his truck, pulled out his keys and drove out of the parking lot.

Merlinda could run.

He would find her tomorrow or the next day.

She wouldn't get away with leaving him.

He would find her and she would regret crossing him.

Tony drove for ten, fifteen, twenty minutes. He didn't see her. She was hiding somewhere.

The two of them would be done when *he* said so. Merlinda didn't call the shots. Tony would never let that happen.

Tony had left the pawn shop in a hurry. He locked the door, but he left the place too fast.

Left it without thinking.

He drove back to the pawn shop and got out of his truck.

Three shadowy figures stepped around him. He hadn't seen them when he pulled in. Two of them pointed shotguns at Tony.

They wore hoods pulled over their heads.

"Put your hands up and we can do this quickly and quietly."

The two holding shotguns were tall.

Tony slowly put his hands in the air. Looked over the shoulder of the closest figure.

A red and white Ford F-150 pickup.

An Indian truck.

He'd seen it around town.

"You won't get away with this, Chief."

He felt a shotgun jab against his ribs.

"Open the door, Tony."

He didn't recognize the voice. The man's voice was hard and low. He didn't sound like any Indian to Tony.

Tony pulled his keys from the front pocket of his jeans.

Opened the front door of the pawn shop.

"Put your hands together."

This time a woman's voice.

Also hard.

She put a plastic zip tie around his hands. Patted him down.

She stood close enough for Tony to smell her body.

The other two were in the shop now.

The woman found the gun he'd slid into his boot. The little derringer he'd bought from the guy driving to California. He'd grabbed it before leaving. Both chambers were loaded. He watched her slide the small gun into her own pocket.

Tony thought about the man from whom he bought the derringer.

Now he felt sorry.

He hoped the guy had gotten his family to California. He hoped the man found a new life there.

He wished he had given the guy a little more money. What the hell was money?

The first man with the shotgun spoke.

"Open that safe, Tony."

Tony knew he had seen the Ford pickup around town. He just couldn't remember where.

The lights in the shop were off, but the man with the shotgun held a BIC lighter up to the dial of the safe.

All Tony could see was the black burlap hood.

All he could feel was the shotgun against the back of his head.

"Open it."

Tony rubbed the first two fingers of his right hand against his thumb.

The safe was an ancient black floor unit, built by the Victor Company of Cincinnati, Ohio at the turn of the century. Tony used it all the time. He heard the click of the casters in the lock when he turned the dial to the last number.

Working the combination with the zip tie holding his wrists together was difficult, but the safe opened.

Tony heard the whistle from the railroad.

He remembered Conover and the day Conover held him near the moving train.

Tony always remembered Conover when he heard the train whistle.

It was the last sound he ever heard.

THE METAL PARTS OF THE SHOTGUN

Locaster watched Dallas put his head into the pawn shop safe.

They had taken their hoods off.

Dallas came out holding stacks of bills in both hands. Surfer boy hadn't been exaggerating. Tony King had money. Maybe not as much as the biker's strip club, but serious money nevertheless. Locaster was back in business. With luck, the plan would continue to work.

Relying this much on Dallas, though, made Locaster nervous. He swung the barrel of the shotgun toward Dallas.

Locaster was pleased with Dallas's reaction.

Surfer boy held the cash, but dropped his jaw.

The grin left his face.

Dallas slowly raised his hands.

"What the hell you think you're doing?" Dallas

said.

"You think I don't know about you and Wanda?"

Dallas said nothing.

Playing it smart for once.

Locaster made a quick jerk with the barrel, keeping it trained on Dallas.

"Wanda, go stand over there with your boyfriend."

Wanda moved close to Dallas.

"Both of you listen. I know what you've been up to. Dallas, you want her so bad, guess what? You got her. Look at her. She's all yours."

Locaster pointed the shotgun at Dallas.

"Wanda, you look at *him*. That's what you got now. Surfer boy's what you got."

Dallas started to say something, but Locaster stopped him.

"There's a price. How much you got saved up, Dallas?"

Dallas's mouth was open like he wanted to say something.

"You want her so bad, you're gonna open the safe at your motel," Locaster said.

He pointed the shotgun at Tony's body.

"Try anything, you end up like this one."

Dallas looked at Tony.

Locaster nodded toward the door of the pawn shop.

"We need to get out of here. How long's the Indian's going to be knocked out?"

"He'll be out for a while, James," Dallas said.

"He's out good."

Locaster looked toward the parking lot. He leaned over Tony's body and brought out a knife. He cut off the plastic ties which held Tony's hands together.

He scooped the ties up and put them in his pocket.

Looked at Dallas.

Even in the dark, Dallas's face looked bad.

"What are you worried about, surfer boy?" Locaster said. "Everything here's copacetic."

The three left the pawn shop and stood in the dark next to Edison's pickup.

Edison was sprawled next to the truck.

Locaster held both shotguns. He wiped down the one he had fired.

Dallas and Wanda stood next to Edison.

Locaster put Edison's hands on the grip and trigger guard.

Rolled Edison's fingers on the metal parts of the shotgun.

Edison moved slightly and groaned.

Locaster touched Edison's face.

He turned toward Dallas and Wanda.

"Get in the car. You two up front. I'll be in the back."

He pointed the shotgun at Dallas.

"You're driving, surfer boy."

Locaster grinned.

"Just make sure you two behave."

PAST THE BUCKET OF BLOOD

Deputy Sheriff Lot Conover fastened the buttons on his cream-colored western shirt one by one. Pulled a pair of his blue jeans from the closet and put them on.

Checked his watch. He was fine.

Late shift. He wouldn't have picked it, but he was helping out. Ledyard and his wife were expecting their baby any time now. Ledyard should be at home with her, especially in the middle of the night.

So he would miss a little sleep. What the hell? Conover lived on naps anyway.

He took down his Zuni bola with the inlaid thunderbird. Slipping it over his head and over his shirt collar, he pulled the slide to the level of the second button of his shirt.

Conover looked around for his glasses. He never used to wear them and he wasn't comfortable with them on. He used to have the vision of a hawk. He didn't like taking the glasses off and putting them on then trying to find them where he left them. These were perplexing matters. One of the things about getting older, he supposed.

Getting older also meant Sheriff Jenkins stuck him with desk duty. Conover was past the normal age for retirement but he wasn't ready to quit.

He pulled on his cowboy boots.

His gun belt and holster, oiled and gleaming, slung over the side of the wooden chair by the washstand. The wooden grip of the Model 10 peeked above the dark leather.

He looked around the living room. The sofa with the newspaper, the lamp and the L'Amour paperback. The curtains his wife had sewn. The glasses were by the Louis L'Amour on the lace cloth covering the small granite topped end table. Just where he'd left them, his wife would have said. He picked up the novel. They would have watched television together last night. She would have made him a snack and given him a kiss before he headed to the complex.

Without Darlene, everything seemed sad. They had made some plans for his retirement, but now he was alone. It had all happened quickly. They had given her six months, but the illness had taken her in much less time than that.

He took the brown paper bag from the refrigerator. He'd prepared himself a snack before going to bed.

He pulled his truck onto the dirt road and looked at the sky.

No moon, plenty of stars.

He drove past the Bucket of Blood before crossing the railroad tracks on his way to the courthouse. The Bucket of Blood and the pawn shop stood near the railroad tracks.

Conover thought about Tony King. The thought came unexpectedly.

He hadn't thought about Tony for years.

Conover remembered scaring the kid.

Edison Graves's truck was parked next to Tony King's pawn shop.

The streets of Holbrook were deserted.

Inside the complex, in the dark interior hall, eight hours stretched in front of him. He had the L'Amour novel. Thank God for that.

Ledyard was ready to go home, Conover could tell. Bustling around, picking up his keys and putting them down again. Ledyard had always been a nervous guy, but Conover was sure Ledyard would eventually make a good sheriff.

"No word yet?" Conover said.

Conover had tried to get Ledyard to run in the last election.

Ledyard paused. "Not yet, Lot. Thanks again, though. It could be any minute."

Ledyard had two older kids and this one on the way. He couldn't afford to make waves. If he had lost the election, he would probably have been out of a job.

Still, he would have made a good sheriff. Better than the current one.

"Anything I need to know?" Conover said. "Anybody in the tank?"

Ledyard shook his head.

"Everything's in it's place, Lot. Nothing's going on. It's quiet. Night went fine."

Lot Conover was always early for his shift. He settled into the wooden chair, pushing to the side the upholstered one Ledyard had brought out from the jury room. Picked up the novel. Something was bothering him. It didn't make any kind of sense. What the hell was Edison's truck doing at that pawn shop?

The next thought was worse.

He'd been so focused on relieving Ledyard, he hadn't investigated it.

He looked around the dark walls of the county complex.

The place could keep for a couple of minutes.

THE DYING ART OF SAFECRACKING

At the Sunset Motel, Dallas pulled the Mercury under the overhang next to the office. The Coupe de Ville was parked at the Ten High. The important thing was Wanda. Wanda was here. Dallas turned to her and smiled. Everything was going just like he'd planned it. The way they had discussed those times on the phone.

Dallas wanted acknowledgment from Wanda. He'd done a good job. A hell of a good job. Everything had worked out easier than he expected.

Locaster was basically turning Wanda over to him.

Dallas looked at her. He was expecting a smile in return. She wasn't smiling. There was no expression on her face at all.

Locaster was holding the shotgun.

Dallas realized that, but there was one thing Locaster didn't know.

Dallas wasn't born yesterday.

Dallas had been smart enough to keep some of his money, even after buying the motel.

Having money in his safe could lead to situations like this. Nobody bothered to crack safes any more. Safecracking was a dying art, like pickpocketing. People didn't want to spend time learning skills. Easier to hold a gun to somebody's head and make them open the safe or empty their wallet.

You never knew who you could trust in life, but Dallas knew he couldn't trust Locaster.

Even after paying for the Sunset with cash, Dallas still had more money.

Mostly for Wanda's benefit, Dallas made a show of unlocking the safe. He wanted to see her reaction to the stacks of cash.

It was real money.

Locaster had blown through his share of the cash and now he held a gun to Dallas. Dallas wondered what would happen if he didn't open the safe. Would Locaster kill him? Leave him on the floor like Tony?

Dallas turned his head around.

Locaster had put the shotgun down.

Dallas spun through the combination.

Wanda stood to the side.

Good girl.

Opening the safe, Dallas looked at the money.

The money was a small price to pay, but he couldn't trust Locaster.

He reached for the first stack of bills.
Handed it to Locaster, who looked at it.
Locaster had lighted another Tiparillo.
"You should leave me some money, James," Dallas said.
Locaster grinned.
"You think that? That's what I should do?"
Dallas's lips were dry.
"I do, James. There's a lot here. I haven't counted it."
Locaster shook his head.
"We can talk about it. Bring out the rest."
Dallas leaned into the safe.
He felt the grip of the Colt.
Locaster thought he was smart. He didn't know Dallas.
Locaster sure as *hell* didn't know Dallas kept a gun in the safe.
Dallas gripped the revolver and slid it back toward himself.

HELL IN ITS DAY

Edison Graves lay on the ground next to his pickup near the Bucket of Blood.

Deputy Lot Conover remembered Edison when he used to tag along behind his older brother.

Livingston Graves was more than just a big brother. Livingston was Edison's surrogate father.

It was a tragedy seeing Livingston Graves go downhill.

Livingston had been proud of Edison. Conover remembered Livingston talking about his brother.

"College man," Livingston had said. "Got his picture in Sports Illustrated, too."

Livingston had been just as smart as his younger brother. Maybe smarter. Probably a better athlete.

They'd had different breaks in life leading them on different paths.

Conover stepped close to Edison's body. He didn't want to see this.

He thought about Livingston's wife, Tasha.

She had practically raised Edison and the other boy who hadn't turned out so well.

Conover knelt by Edison.

Edison was breathing.

His head had suffered some damage. There was blood on the back of his head.

In the back of the pickup, a shotgun lay in the bed.

Conover didn't touch it.

The Bucket of Blood Saloon.

Closed permanently, but hell in it's day.

Conover smelled Edison's breath.

Alcohol, but not overwhelming. He looked at the bloody patch on the back of Edison's head.

Somebody had knocked him out.

From behind.

Conover went to his truck and pulled out a wool blanket and spread it over Edison's body. Patted his shoulder.

He was going to need to call somebody.

He saw Edison's eye open.

DIRTY MONEY

Locaster stood behind Dallas.

Locaster thumbed through the first stack of bills. Impressive, but less than he expected.

Dallas had his head in the safe. He was coming out.

Locaster heard the scrape. Not loud, but loud enough.

Locaster could read Dallas like a book.

Dallas was going to play hero.

Locaster had seen the look on Dallas when he had put the shotgun down. He was tempted to wait for surfer boy's big dumb face to come out of the safe holding whatever piece he'd stashed in there.

Locaster was tempted, but not foolish.

The first shot from Locaster's Cobra hit Dallas under the shoulder. Locaster continued firing until Dallas dropped completely onto the linoleum floor.

Locaster put the Cobra on top of the safe.

He'd fired all the cartridges.

Dallas was good and dead.

Smoke rose from Locaster's Tiparillo.

Locaster looked at Wanda. She had a strange look on her face.

She wasn't looking at Locaster. She was looking at the money.

"Take this for a sec, Wanda. Locaster handed her the grubby stack of fives, tens, and twenties.

Dirty money. Probably rentals from the motel units.

Wanda took the money from Locaster.

Locaster pushed Dallas over with his boot and leaned into the safe.

Dallas's gun fell out of his hand.

"Look here," Locaster said.

He pointed at the back of the safe.

"We got more down in back."

One more stack of bills.

Probably the same amount as the first.

He grabbed the stack and turned around.

The derringer Wanda held was a tiny thing and Locaster didn't see the two barrels Wanda held between his eyes.

He wasn't able to speak before she fired.

ADOBE WALLS AND PLYWOOD ON THE WINDOWS

In Edison's dream, Deputy Lot Conover took him down to the cell. The deputy's hand shielded Edison's head so it wouldn't scrape the low doorway of the lock-up. In the dream, Livingston was with Edison. He hadn't died yet. Livingston was saying something about the jail smelling like Pine-Sol.

Livingston walked down the step with Edison. He was describing the gray galvanized walls of the jail cell and the big drawing of the Virgen de Guadalupe.

Livingston left when the bars of the cell opened and Edison felt somebody shaking him.

Was he smelling a wood fire?

Even without moving a muscle or opening his eyes, he could tell he was outside on the ground.

Something had happened to his head.

He didn't know where he was or how long he'd been there.

He wasn't ready to face the pain he knew he would feel opening his eyes.

Edison had been thrown from bulls and hit by linemen but this pain was different.

He braced his head.

Somebody was with him.

He heard a slow, cadenced voice.

"Easy there, Edison. Easy. Keep your eyes closed."

Edison was sweating. His jeans and western shirt were caked with the same dusty grime covering his body.

"Dang," he said, "dang."

He felt like he'd been kicked by a horse.

A hangover was nothing compared to this.

He pulled out his bandanna.

Wiped sweat from his face. He didn't dare touch his skull

Pain radiated through his body.

He opened his eyes.

Deputy Lot Conover leaned over him.

A blanket covered Edison's body.

Edison's eyes adjusted to the dark. He knew where he was.

Concrete dinosaurs. Railroad tracks.

Lurching to his knees he threw up.

The pain in his head was immediate, then subsided.

Edison got to his knees and staggered toward the saloon.

Conover walked next to him, guiding his steps.

How had he gotten here?

The Bucket of Blood Saloon. Adobe walls and plywood covering long shattered windows.

Across from the saloon, lights came from the windows and open front door of Tony King's pawn shop.

"What the hell happened to you?"

Conover's voice.

Edison didn't have an answer.

He'd had a couple of drinks. That was it.

After Merlinda was gone, things had gotten hazy.

What the hell happened to the back of his skull?

"Somebody drugged me," Edison said.

He passed out again.

❉ ❉ ❉

It was pitch black.

Edison saw the branches of the mesquite tree.

Skeletons waving their arms at him.

He slapped the back pocket of his jeans.

Conover was looking at his head.

His wallet was in his jeans. Edison pulled it out. He still had money and the Arizona driver's license with his Tucson address listed.

"You got clobbered, son," Conover said.

Edison shook his head.

It would take a while to bring things back into focus.

※ ※ ※

The shotgun lay across the bed of the truck.

Edison put the wallet back in his pocket then eased himself down again, level with the ground, pointing his face away from the truck and in the direction of the saloon.

D-I-V-O-R-C-E

The little band didn't have a girl singer. Even so, the guy with the Telecaster and red beard insisted Forrest Canyon play the Tammy Wynette song.

D-I-V-O-R-C-E.

A two hankie song if Forrest had ever heard one. The song's intro was Forrest on the Sho-Bud.

The guitar player had changed the lyrics telling the story from the husband's point of view. He wasn't half bad, but he was no Tammy Wynette.

Forrest Canyon didn't want to wait for morning before heading out of town. The Pontiac had maybe half a tank of gas and fresh oil. He didn't need some grease monkey giving him any bull about the dark exhaust pluming from the tailpipe. Forrest knew he was burning oil. Any idiot could see that.

Forrest planned to get to Flagstaff in a couple of hours. He would gas up, put in some *more* 10W-40 and a little bottle of Marvel Mystery Oil.

Then he would be ready to cross the desert to Bakersfield.

He would think things over in the coffee shop of the Flagstaff Little America.

He had stayed at Little America once while on tour. Forrest remembered the place. Big red vinyl booths and friendly waitresses. He pulled out his eelskin wallet and thumbed through the bills the big guitar player had given him. He could tell at a glance the payment was more than fair.

Maybe he wouldn't wait to eat until Flag. He could get something to eat just as easily in Winslow which was up the road maybe an hour away.

Forrest was comfortable in his Sears Ted Williams bag. He felt cozy with the pillow he'd taken from a motel in Shreveport.

He had parked the Pontiac out of sight behind a road sign advertising a rock and mineral shop and had barely fallen asleep when the whistle from the train woke him up.

He knew he wouldn't get back to sleep.

There was no reason to linger in this town.

His money makers, the steel guitar and the Fender amp were safely stowed in the back of the Pontiac where he had packed them.

He remembered the big guitar player shaking his hand like crazy.

"Man, you got a job with us, no matter how long you can stay," the guitar player said.

He pointed at the Sho-Bud.

"You make that thing flat-out sing."

Forrest looked at his reflection in the rear-view mirror. Pulled his comb from the Jack of Diamonds pocket of his shirt. Opening the glove compartment, he pushed his gun to the side and grabbed his tube of Brylcreem. Forrest worked a dab of it through his dark hair, restoring his pompadour.

He cruised the Pontiac through the streets of the sleeping town.

Not a half bad place.

It would be tempting to stay. He always felt that way leaving places.

In a couple of days, though, he would be in Bakersfield, and he would have forgotten all about Holbrook.

Forrest switched on the high beams and looked at the sign.

Route 66.

Every town looked good in the rear-view mirror.

THE HITCHHIKER

Conover knew Edison hadn't killed Tony.

Edison's head had been cracked, and he was lucky to be alive.

He'd seen the open door of the pawn shop and walked in.

Tony King was dead, sprawled beside his empty safe.

Half his head gone from a shotgun blast. More than likely the gun in back of Edison's truck had been used.

Whoever had done it wanted to set Edison up.

❈ ❈ ❈

"What brought you up here, Edison?"

Conover helped Edison into the cab of his F-150. The keys were in the ignition of Edison's truck.

Edison shook his head.

"I don't know," he said.

"Think," Conover said. "Why are you here?"

"Rodeo," Edison said. "Dallas King called me and told me about it."

Speaking took it's toll. Edison's head lolled to the side onto his right shoulder.

Conover pushed Edison into the passenger's seat. There was no way Edison could drive or do much else right now.

"I'm taking you somewhere," Conover said.

❊ ❊ ❊

The bed in Conover's guest bedroom was made up.

Conover helped Edison on top of the covers and put the blanket over his body.

Trail's End hung on the wall. The painting of the Indian on horseback would be the first thing Edison saw when he awakened.

He would live.

Edison was tough. Just like Livingston.

Conover turned off the lamp and left the room.

He had made the telephone calls when he got to his house. The pawn shop would be swarming by now. The sheriff could take it from here. There would be explaining to do, but nothing Conover couldn't handle. He went out the front door and got back into the cab of Edison's truck.

Edison would live.

❊ ❊ ❊

Conover checked his watch. He could hear sirens on the other side of town. He needed to go back over there.

Parking Edison's truck next to the Stagecoach Steak House, Conover looked at the Sunset Motel across Route 66 then checked his Model 10.

Dallas would be in there.

Possibly with the shotgun.

The lights were on in the office, but there was no sign of life.

In front of the motel a woman stood in the street with a big Samsonite and a smaller makeup case.

A young blonde woman.

It's a free country, Conover thought. She's headed out of town.

The streetlight and the motel neon bathed the woman in an other-worldly glow.

The blonde woman's thumb was out.

She wouldn't have to wait long for a ride.

Conover needed backup. He dug in his pocket and pulled out some change for the pay phone outside the Stagecoach.

A truck passed, and another one slowed down next to the hitchhiker.

The second truck kept going.

Standing under the sign for the Sunset Motel, the woman threw her head back.

She was alone.

The sun would come up soon.

Conover watched a dark blue Pontiac make a

slow stop. Black smoke billowed from the back.

A man with a black pompadour rolled the driver-side window down.

He said something to the woman.

She got in the car.

Tennessee license plates.

Conover made a note of the numbers.

* * *

Conover and the sheriff looked at the two bodies lying near the open safe.

The office of the Sunset was covered with blood.

They both knew the big man with the blood stained guayaberra. Everybody knew Dallas King.

The sheriff looked at Conover.

"You pretty sure he was the one killed his cousin?"

Conover nodded.

"One of them did, anyhow."

"You recognize the other one?"

Conover looked. The other man was even taller than Dallas King and he wore a bloodsoaked beige leisure suit with a pack of Tiparillos stuck in his breast pocket.

Conover shook his head.

"Never seen him, before. I don't think he's from here."

He turned to the sheriff.

"Sheriff," Conover said. "You need to get on the

horn and put out an all-points."

The sheriff looked at him.

"Dark blue Pontiac LeMans. Late sixties model," Conover said. "Tennessee license plates. Heading west."

He gave the numbers to the sheriff.

"There's a woman in the car. She may be armed and dangerous."

BAKERSFIELD

Wanda had one shot left in the derringer.

She could pull the weapon out any time.

The twin barrels were fitted over and under. The hinge was simple like the shotguns Locaster let her fire.

Pull the barrel down and load the cartridges.

Snap it up and it's ready to fire.

Easy peasy. The first round had been a skinny shotgun shell.

Locaster would have found it necessary to explain.

"That's a *slug*," he would have said about the round which killed him.

"It's not *shot*."

She looked at the driver.

He was smiling slightly and tapping his hands on the steering wheel.

❋ ❋ ❋

The driver didn't talk at first. That was good.

She recognized him. He played steel guitar in

the band last night.

Last night?

It had been only a few hours ago.

She couldn't mistake him.

The pompadour.

The jack of diamonds on his pocket.

The comb.

He was going to Bakersfield.

Happy to give her a ride as far as she wanted.

She looked at the speedometer.

Cruising along just below sixty.

Poky.

"Bakersfield is one hell of a city," the man said.

Wanda nodded.

"You want to put your things in the trunk?"

"That's all right," Wanda said.

Wanda clutched the Samsonite between her legs and kept the makeup case on her lap.

She watched the road.

The mountains in the distance could barely be seen in the dark.

The driver looked over at her.

Liked what he saw and smiled.

She was tired.

Too tired to give her cheerleader smile.

She knew better than to fall asleep.

"My name's Forrest," he said.

THE DESERTED MIDWAY OF THE COUNTY FAIRGROUND

By noon, the sun was shining brightly again. On the deserted midway of the county fairground, Edison walked alone. He thought about Merlinda and the time he'd spent with her last night. Merlinda and he had both grown up in the time he'd been away.

Then he thought about what Deputy Conover told him.

His head felt bad, but Deputy Conover made coffee, bacon, and eggs.

It was strange waking up and not knowing where he was, but Conover's house was comfortable, and Edison hadn't felt any uneasiness.

Merlinda and he had both been in their teens when they first met. They weren't teenagers now.

Edison had a regular job in the mine when it opened again. He had a degree to finish and a concha belt.

He needed to find Merlinda. He would help her if she wanted his help.

"Go find her, Edison," Conover said. "You and I both know where she is. You don't do that, you'll wonder about it the rest of your life."

Edison walked along the midway like he'd done a hundred times as a teenager. Empty booths which in the fall would hold carnival games.

He reached the end of the midway where the rides were operated. Rides like Dallas's Tilt-a-Whirl.

Conover had told him Dallas was dead.

He kept walking to the rodeo grounds. This was where he'd first competed. Edison remembered his first ride and the pride he felt hearing his name announced on the loud speaker.

This was the first place Merlinda saw him ride a bronc. Livingston had brought him here. Livingston taught him how to take a fall and get back up. He taught him by showing him how to do it.

Livingston was a hell of a cowboy. Everybody agreed on that. Maybe the best cowboy this town had ever seen.

Edison remembered Livingston looking at him when Edison used to talk about things over the rainbow and far away.

"Don't tell me about *there*, mister," Livingston said, "not when you don't know about *here*, yet."

Livingston told Edison about his visions.

Edison thought about his older brother. You could see the visions in Livingston's eyes if you looked for them.

❊ ❊ ❊

The fairgrounds were hot. The only shade provided by empty exhibition halls.

Edison remembered going with Merlinda to the county fair when they were in high school.

It had been in the middle of September. He remembered looking at jars of beans and salsa, arrangements of dried flowers, agricultural machinery.

An Elvis impersonator had performed. This hadn't been too long after Presley's death. The man with the black wig and sideburns sweated his way through *Suspicious Minds*. At the end of the song, he took one of his orange scarfs and put it around Merlinda's neck. The man was even more overweight than Elvis had been at the end. The impersonator lingered with the scarf and looked at Merlinda just a little longer than necessary.

Merlinda had been in high school then.

Maybe the same age Priscilla had been when Elvis met her.

Edison got Merlinda away from the guy pretty quick.

❊ ❊ ❊

Conover told Edison about the chase on the highway between Joseph City and Winslow.

The guy hadn't wanted to stop.

Did Edison remember the guy with the Jack of Diamonds on his shirt?

The steel guitar player thought *he* was the one who was going to jail.

As if the sheriff would have blocked the highway because some guy had picked up a hooker.

Conover laughed telling Edison the story.

That was the good news. The woman was now in custody, and she'd told a hell of a story before she got lawyered up.

The steel guitar player's name was Forrest Canyon.

"How about that for a name?" Conover said. "Sounds like a comic strip hero."

Forrest Canyon was one lucky son-of-a-gun.

"Turns out Wanda had another shot in her derringer. First one, she used on her husband. She's claiming self-defense."

Edison nodded. Sipped the coffee. Taking in the fact of Dallas's death.

"Forrest Canyon could have gotten himself dead, too," Conover said. "She woulda said *that* was self-defense, too."

Conover made more coffee while Edison looked out Conover's window. A beautiful day.

He wouldn't be going to Indian Wells.

"Poor old Dallas," Conover had said. "He never was exactly bright. But in this case, I'd say he got himself in with *exactly* the wrong company."

❋ ❋ ❋

Horses were kept in the fairground stables year round. The dark interior kept the temperature cooler than outside where Calvin Barnes took the horses for exercise.

❋ ❋ ❋

"You know where she'll be," Conover said.

Edison nodded. He knew where Merlinda would go.

After running away from Tony King she would go where she felt safe.

Conover was right.

❋ ❋ ❋

Nobody was in the stables except Calvin.

Calvin was always there in bib overalls and muck boots.

Calvin knew everybody in town.

"Edison Graves," Calvin said.

Just as if he'd seen him yesterday afternoon.

"You come up here for the rodeo?"

Edison pulled up his jeans.

"Supposed to. But I gotta check on this horse now."

"Which horse?"

Edison pointed vaguely down the barn.

"Merlinda's."

Calvin's smile exposed a row of tobacco stained teeth.

He pointed.

"Third stall on the left."

It didn't take long to get the horse cinched and saddled.

"Glad it's you, Edison," Calvin said. "That one's got spirit."

Edison patted the horse and whispered into her ear.

He would ride her back to Merlinda.

Edison swung onto the back of the horse. Riding was natural for Edison.

The paint was beautiful and she did have spirit.

She snorted and reared when Edison wheeled her out of the barn and into the heat of the sun.

Edison knew where to find Merlinda.

THE PAINT

Crossing the interstate east of town with the sun dropping in the sky behind him, Edison felt a chill. The paint held her head up. She was ready to keep going. Edison wasn't riding her hard and they weren't going too far.

Edison rode north from the fairground, skirting the town. He looked down at the horse and the saddle.

Dallas had tried to set him up.

He had called Edison, supposedly to get him to ride in Indian Wells.

Dallas even dragged Merlinda into his plan. He must have tricked her some way. Otherwise, she never would have come to the Ten High.

Somehow, Tony King found out Merlinda was at the bar. Probably Dallas told him.

Dallas had set Edison up for murder.

Without Conover, Edison could be in a jail cell right now, waiting for a lawyer to untangle a web of circumstantial evidence pointing to his guilt.

As if Edison would have killed Tony King.

Conover said they had used a shotgun on Tony King. Either Dallas or his partner had done it.

Maybe even the girl.

Edison remembered the way Livingston's blood spread across the carpet at the Sunset Motel.

Edison would never have killed Tony.

He didn't want to kill anyone.

"Whatever you do, don't kill your brother," Livingston once said.

Edison remembered the way Livingston said it and remembered wondering what Livingston meant.

Livingston had laughed, looking at Edison.

"You know what?" Livingston said. "They're all your brother."

Then Livingston himself had been killed in as ugly a way as Edison could imagine.

* * *

Edison could have taken his Ford to find Merlinda. Riding her horse made more sense. It might not make sense to everyone, but it would make sense to the important people.

Livingston would have understood.

Conover would understand.

Edison looked at the setting sun.

He wasn't far from where he needed to go.

He touched the paint's reins.

Merlinda would understand.

ENCHILADAS

Deputy Sheriff Lot Conover ordered his usual plate of sour cream enchiladas served with grilled onions and frijoles. He waited for the dish to come to the table before sipping the black coffee. Shotguns were used for both crimes. Forensics would confirm that, but nobody but a class-A idiot would think there would be any surprises in that report. The evidence was splattered on the walls of both the pawn shop and the motel office. The tricky part would be estimating the time between the two deaths, but even that wouldn't take long. Even *that* wouldn't make much difference. Already, Wanda had a lawyer over from Flagstaff. The guy had appeared out of nowhere, briefcase in hand. Everybody knew the Flagstaff lawyer. He would get Wanda the best deal he could.

First he would have Wanda recant her confession which he would say was coerced.

Simple, when you thought about it.

Hadn't Tony King made a stir when he went into the Ten High last night?

Tony had been alive then. He was dead now, and Conover felt a little older today. Conover had seen

Dallas King yesterday, hadn't he?

Riding around town in his big Cadillac like King Shit, asking about Merlinda Beach.

Juanita brought the chips to the table and put the two kinds of salsa down next to them.

"That's it for now, honey?"

Conover looked up.

Juanita gave him a wink.

He had been busy thinking. The wink surprised him.

"You let me know if you need anything else."

Juanita was just slightly south of Conover's sixty years.

"Might like a little more water, Juanita."

Somebody had started the jukebox.

Marty Robbins singing *El Paso*.

Conover liked the song, but this situation was a whole lot more compelling.

Two, no *three* homicides in Holbrook on the same night.

Holbrook hadn't lost much with the death of either Dallas King or Tony King.

As a matter of fact, using the law of addition by subtraction, the town would be improved by their absence.

Still, this wasn't the old west, and Holbrook wasn't ruled by the gun anymore.

But there was still a place for Conover.

There would always be a place for men like Conover.

❊ ❊ ❊

The enchiladas came.

Juanita put them down in front of Conover and smiled at him. Conover looked at her again. There was something about Juanita he hadn't noticed. He would have to think about that.

The enchies were just the way he liked them with melted cheese floating in the grilled onions. Across the restaurant, Juanita stood fanning herself with a menu.

He would have to think about that.

He sipped his ice tea.

Dug into the enchiladas.

A PLUME OF SMOKE

The sheep were spread out over the horizon.
White on a field of ocher.

In the distance, Joe Beach's house stood with a plume of smoke coming from the chimney.

The scene reminded Edison of a child's drawing. Something to put on the refrigerator.

Here are the mountains. Here are the sheep. Here is a hogan with smoke coming from the chimney.

Edison touched his heels to the horse and made his way around the milling flock

A fence of T-bars and baling wire ran in front of the hogan. A dog was barking. An old Ford Pinto with a Northern Arizona University sticker in the back window was parked next to the hogan.

It had to be Merlinda's car. Joe didn't drive.

The old man sat next to the front steps on an aluminum lawn chair. He wore an old field jacket. Blue jeans. A red bandanna was tied around his head.

Dark glasses.

Joe Beach was legally blind. He would have heard the horse approach and the dog barking.

Merlinda would be inside the hogan, probably looking at Edison right now through one of the windows.

Edison kept his horse at a distance until the old man signaled for Edison to come forward.

"Joe," Edison said. "It's me, Edison Graves."

Edison watched a smile cross Joe's face.

"I'm looking for Merlinda."

"She said you came back, Edison. You know I can't see that good now. I had to make sure you weren't the other one."

Edison saw the .44 in Joe's lap for the first time.

The old man would have been ready if Tony King had followed Merlinda.

Tony's last view of the earth would have been a pasture full of sheep.

The door opened.

PERMISSION

Merlinda came out from the hogan.

She wore a long pleated velvet skirt, a mustard colored blouse, the squash blossom necklace from her mother's family.

She was beautiful.

It was the golden hour. The sky had turned a honey color around Merlinda.

"I knew you'd get here," she said.

She walked out a few more steps.

Merlinda stood in front of her grandfather and held her hands out to Edison.

The old man coughed. He put the gun into his holster.

"Looks like you found her, Edison. Now what you gonna do?"

Edison looked at the old man.

What could he say to Joe Beach?

He needed to choose his words carefully.

"Grandfather," Edison said. "I'd like your permission to talk to Merlinda."

❋ ❋ ❋

Edison held her hands while the sky darkened. They both waited for Joe Beach's response.

For several minutes, the old man didn't answer.

He looked at Edison and he looked at Merlinda.

The paint whinnied.

Edison felt Merlinda's hands in his own.

The man cleared his throat.

"Go ahead and talk to her, Edison. I've known you all your life. You have my permission."

Edison felt Merlinda squeeze his hand.

The old man continued.

"But if you take her away from here, remember this."

Edison turned to listen.

"You will need to come back for me," the old man said.

Joe Beach waited.

The sky had turned purple and red.

Finally the old man spoke again.

"Come back for me when the time comes."

McIndoe Falls, Vermont
March 2020

BOOKS BY THIS AUTHOR

Trinity Works Alone

Trinity Thinks Twice

Trinity And The Short-Timer

Trinity Springs Forward

Ferguson's Trip

ACKNOWLEDGEMENT

Thanks go to my wife, retired Navajo County Superior Court Judge Carolyn C. Holliday, who knows Holbrook and Navajo County well. Thank you Carolyn for your careful reading of this book at several stages.

Also, thanks to Larry Ratcliff of L.R. Investigations in Pinetop-Lakeside, Arizona for explaining certain technical details pertaining to firearms.

Finally, thanks to you for reading this book.

If you enjoyed *Dim Lights Thick Smoke*, please consider writing a short review and telling your friends. As Walter Tevis, writer of *The Hustler* and *The Queen's Gambit* wrote when making the same request: "word of mouth is an author's best friend and much appreciated."

Trevor Holliday

Printed in Great Britain
by Amazon